WE HAUNT THESE WOODS

HOLLEY CORNETTO

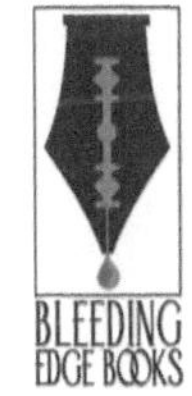

BLEEDING EDGE BOOKS

WE HAUNT THESE WOODS
Copyright © 2022 by Holley Cornetto
All Rights Reserved

ISBN: 979-8-218-05090-0
Cover artwork by Greg Chapman | Dark-Designs.com
Book design & formatting by Todd Keisling | Dullington Design Co.

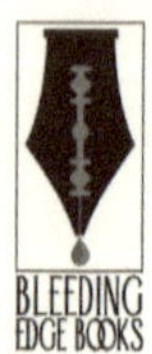

Bleeding Edge Books
www.bleedingedgepub.com

To Mom,
I think you really would have loved this one

WE HAUNT THESE WOODS

PROLOGUE

Tell me what you remember."

Jennifer sat across from me in a booth at the Tick Tock Diner. It was past midnight, and the place was mostly deserted. A jukebox stood in the corner, covered in dust. With its faded orange seating and cracked gray linoleum, the whole place looked like a relic of the past; maybe that was why I'd chosen it for our reunion.

I'd tried not to think about her for years, and mostly succeeded, until that picture popped up on my social media feed with the header *People You May Know*. She'd changed, that was certain, but I still recognized her. That photo stirred feelings long dormant within me. Feelings I thought I'd left behind. Imagine my surprise when not only did she remember me, but agreed to meet. I hadn't planned on talking about the past. She had brought it up first.

"Nate!"

The urgency of her tone brought me back to the world, back to the moment.

"Yeah?"

"Tell me what you remember."

I swallowed hard, considering my answer. How much did I remember? How much of what I thought I knew was real?

"I remember the night at the bonfire, when we found out about Franklin. I had a crush on you. Did you know that? I was nervous." I looked away, feeling a rush of heat on my cheeks.

I'd thought the confession would be easy, and that we could just laugh it off, but there was something in that look she gave me. Something there that reminded me of the old Jennifer, and of the ways things used to be.

But she wasn't the old Jennifer, not anymore. She had so many piercings in her face, she resembled a pincushion. From the looks of it, her hair had once been blue, but was now faded to green from neglect. She was still beautiful, no doubt, but the last twenty years hadn't been kind. My stomach fluttered. I'd been so anxious about seeing her again that I hadn't been able to eat. I'd just paced around most of the day, drinking coffee, wondering who she'd become, and what she'd think of me now that we were older. Maybe that's how it was with first crushes. Maybe, deep down, you always felt a spark.

"What else?" She turned to the seat beside her, rummaging through her oversized purse until she pulled out a prescription pill bottle. She shook a pill into her hand and swallowed it without water.

"The song," I muttered, drifting far away. "I can't forget that song."

CHAPTER 1

I'd never realized growing up how privileged I'd been, sheltered from problems like divorce, bankruptcy, or negligent parents. My childhood had been near perfect; one that others might envy. Every summer when I was young, my family visited our cabin at Lake Swart, tucked up in the foothills of northern New Jersey. The water there was pristine, the bluest blue I'd ever seen, and the shore was covered in bone-white sand. There were fourteen lake cabins in our little community, and in any given summer, most of them were occupied. It was the same families every year, and we got to know each other well during those summers together.

It was tradition for our parents to throw a beach party the first night at the lake. They spent the evening drinking beer, and we made s'mores. It was when everyone caught up with each other, and all that we'd missed since last summer. S'more night was legendary.

My twelfth year at the lake, the bonfire was blazing

again, sending up smoke and debris that twirled through the evening sky. The whole beach was illuminated. From the boombox by the folding chairs a DJ promised to play "all the hits from the seventies, eighties, and today." A big red cooler, half buried in the sand, was so full of Bud Lite and Pepsi that the lid wouldn't close.

Families started to trickle in. Brandon arrived first, wearing a Crimson Tide hat and cargo pants. His pockets were already bulging, no doubt from whatever rocks he'd collected along the way. He was tall and lanky, with dark eyes and skin.

Brandon was an Eagle Scout, a living embodiment of the old Boy Scouts motto: *Be prepared.* He fancied himself a cartographer, always drawing maps and doing calculations. Although I couldn't see it, I was sure he was wearing his prized possession— the compass necklace he'd gotten last year for his birthday. He walked over and sat on the rock nearest me, holding out a hand. We gave each other five, up high, down low, and this time I was too slow as he jerked his hand away. It wasn't quite a secret handshake, but we got a good laugh out of it.

Lee joined us at the circle next. He was older than the rest of the lake kids, making him our leader by default. He wore a red bandana and a Van Halen t-shirt with a lollipop tucked behind his ear like a cigarette, and a Walkman clipped on his belt buckle. Lee was a rebel, and a troublemaker. He reeked of cigarette smoke and danger, and we all followed his cues. He stood with his foot propped on a rock, across the fire from us. "Check this out," he said, turning to show off the rat tail he'd grown out. It went down past his shoulders, but it was better than the mullet he'd had the year before.

Brandon shrugged. "Cool, I guess."

Lee opened his mouth to say something else, but was interrupted when Sarah and Jennifer arrived. Though sisters, they were opposites. Sarah, the older of the two, was tall and loud. She liked makeup and manicures, and by the way she looked at him, she also liked Lee. She wore sandals that were too fancy to be out in the sand and a pair of rolled up denim cutoffs. I wasn't fooled, those shorts had probably cost more than my entire closet's worth of clothes.

Jennifer was short and shy with long dark hair to her waist, and bangs that hung down across her forehead. When she laughed, she covered her mouth with her hand. I wondered if this would be the summer that I told her I loved her. Jennifer sat on the rock beside me. My stomach fluttered.

Marcus, the youngest of our summer regulars, arrived last, and a collective groan went out from the group.

"Oh great. The loser's back," Lee sighed.

"Aww, come on. He isn't so bad," I replied. Marcus was unapologetically a dork. He loved science fiction and fantasy and was practically obsessed with *The X-Files* and conspiracy theories.

Brandon opened the box of graham crackers and passed them around. "I heard Franklin's family isn't coming this year."

I looked around the group. None of the others reacted. "What happened?" I asked.

"I dunno, his family moved, or something?" Brandon

answered, unwrapping a chocolate bar. "They won't be back this summer, or maybe ever." He passed the chocolate to me.

"That sucks." I broke off a block and passed it to Jennifer. I blushed when her hand brushed mine, and I wondered if she had a boyfriend.

"That isn't what happened," Marcus said, taking the seat to my left.

"Shut up, Dorkus. Nobody cares what you think," Sarah snapped.

Lee leaned forward, feigning interest. "Well come on, weirdo, what'd you think happened?"

I knew where this was going. Lee was looking for fuel, something he could use to tease Marcus for the rest of the summer, and that dope Marcus was dumb enough to give it to him.

Marcus cleared his throat, speaking in conspiratorial tones. "He vanished. They never found him."

"Bullshit." Lee tossed a marshmallow. It bounced off Marcus and into the flames.

Brandon shifted uncomfortably, removing his hat and using it to wipe the sweat from his brow. "Marcus, that's messed up dude. Why do you always have to go there with your creepy-ass shit? His family moved, that's all."

Marcus shook his head and brushed graham cracker crumbs off his *I Want to Believe* t-shirt. "I know it's true, because he went missing here, at the lake."

"No way." Jennifer speared a marshmallow and held it over the fire, watching as the outside turned black.

"Yes way," Marcus continued. "It was in the paper. He lived in Greenbriar, one town over from me."

The fire popped, and Jennifer gasped. I placed my hand on top of hers and smiled. I tried to look reassuring, but I was pretty sure I looked like a giant dweeb.

Lee scoffed. "This is the dumbest shit I've ever heard. If he went missing at the lake, we would've known about it." He pulled a white Bic from his pocket and struck it, holding the flame beneath his skewered marshmallow. He was showing off, I knew. The marshmallow caught fire; he laughed and blew out the flame.

Marcus frowned at the lighter. I knew what he was thinking: it was likely swiped from Lee's parents. Lee teased him mercilessly last summer for being a narc. Marcus looked away from the lighter and went back to telling his story. "My family and his were the last ones here, remember? You were all gone by then. The police came and everything. They even asked me questions about where he was, and when I'd seen him last. It was the coolest thing that's ever happened to me." Sensing his excitement had gotten the better of him, Marcus lowered his head and added, "Except for Franklin going missing, I mean."

"How would you know anything, dweeb?" Lee flicked a bit of hot marshmallow at Marcus.

"Because after you guys left, we hung out in the woods. We found this cave down by the Boulder Path that...was weird." His face screwed up into a perplexed look.

Jennifer inspected her toasted marshmallow. "A hidden

cave? That sounds neat. I want to see it." She took a bite from her s'more. Melted chocolate dripped down her chin, and I shivered.

"Me too!" I said, a little too quickly. "Why don't we meet up in the morning, by the path?"

"We'll all go," Lee announced, decision made. "And when we don't find anything, I'm going to toss you in the lake, freak." I hoped he meant Marcus, but he was looking at me when he said it.

CHAPTER 2

What about you?" I asked, trying to get a look at the label on her pill bottle.

"I don't remember what I don't remember. Sounds stupid, right? My parents put me into therapy after that summer. You probably didn't know that. They put me on so many goddamn pills that I can't tell the real from the nightmares anymore." She ran a hand through her disheveled hair with chipped black fingernails chewed to the quick. I felt a stab of guilt as my eyes wandered up her arm, looking for track marks. Nothing. If she was using, at least she wasn't shooting up. Maybe the prescriptions were enough.

I nodded, trying not to meet her eyes. "I had nightmares, too. I kept dreaming about Franklin's face, and Marcus... sometimes I still dream about them." I couldn't bring myself to mention Sarah. Not yet.

"Did you ever go back to the lake?" She fidgeted in the seat, looking uncomfortable in her own skin.

I was overwhelmed with the sudden desire to put my

arm around her and tell her I'd be there for her, that I'd see her through. But that was the reflex of a young boy who still believed in gallantry, and we weren't twelve years old anymore. In the years past, I'd learned not to make promises I couldn't keep. "No. My family sold our cabin after that summer. Too many bad memories."

Strips of shredded napkin drifted onto the table. The movement was automatic; she didn't even seem aware she was doing it. Faded white lines scarred her wrist. I didn't need to ask what'd caused them. It was to be expected, after all we'd gone through. We'd all had it bad, but it was worse for her. I'd known when I reached out to her that she wouldn't be that same young girl anymore, how could she have been? But I hadn't expected something so damaged and fragile where the girl I'd loved had once been.

She fidgeted with an unopened pack of Camels. "Look, I have to know. No, I *need* to know. Was the cave real?"

CHAPTER 3

The next morning, we met at the Boulder Path, an unmarked trail leading away from the beach deeper into the forest. We'd given it the nickname because it was littered with glacial erratics. We used them for climbing, or hide-and-seek before Lee declared it to be a baby game and forbade us from playing. Franklin and I defied him once, but when Lee found out he gave us wedgies that made my balls sore for days.

Despite no official trail markers or blazes to identify the path, it was well-trodden and easy enough to follow with only a minimal amount of bushwhacking. The previous summer, Brandon had drawn up crude maps of the various paths through the forest, taking care to mark places where snake dens and poison ivy lingered.

I carried a backpack full of granola bars and trail mix, and the canteen I'd gotten for my birthday was strapped around my shoulder. Jennifer and Sarah were already there, Sarah tapping her foot impatiently, and Jennifer watching for the rest of us to arrive.

Ever the Scout, Brandon's compass and whistle hung from his pack. He pulled out the maps he'd drawn while Marcus diligently pointed out the vague direction of his mystery cave. Lee was last to arrive at the rendezvous point, not carrying any supplies. Not that he ever did.

We entered the forest and followed the trail past the usual places. Eventually Marcus wandered off the beaten path, heading farther into the woods. "It's this way, over by that hill." He pointed through a patch of trees and boulders, but I couldn't see the hill from where I stood.

Sarah stopped, brushing off the front of her blouse. "I'm not going any farther."

Lee tugged her arm. "Come on, Sarah. If Frog-Face says it's over here, then that's where we're going."

She shook her head, jerking her arm away. "You go ahead, but I'm staying here. I'm not going to get my clothes all dirty in the weeds and muck. These are *Tommy Hilfiger.* One thorn could ruin this entire outfit."

Lee glared at her. "Anyone else want to chicken out? Now's your big chance. Anyone?"

"I'm not chicken. And anyway, excuse me for giving a crap about how I look."

He ignored her, turning to the rest of us. No one responded. "Just Sarah? Good." Lee sneered at her. "Have fun by yourself, chickenshit."

Sarah huffed and rolled her eyes, turning back down the path toward the cabins.

The rest of us followed Marcus deeper into the forest, dead leaves crunching under our feet as we marched on.

Vines snaked up large oaks, and the undergrowth was dense and tangled. We all grew silent in anticipation of something we couldn't name. Brandon produced a thick piece of yellow chalk from one of his many pockets, and marked the largest oaks as we passed. "So we can find our back here again if we need to," he explained.

"Good idea," Jennifer said.

I felt my face burn and wished I thought of it "Yeah, Brandon. Good idea."

The forest grew thicker around us. I'd never been this far off the path before. Briars snagged at the leg of my pants, and no birds or insects chirped around us. The only noise was the crunching of leaves as we trekked on. Uneasy, I decided to break the silence. "How did you find this place, anyway?"

Marcus shrugged. "Franklin showed it to me. We were here for a week after you guys left, so we had a lot of time to explore."

"He didn't mention how he found it?" I asked.

"I didn't ask. I mean, we're in the woods all the time. I guess he just found it while he was out here," Marcus replied.

I wondered why Franklin would've wandered off the path alone. He wasn't like Brandon, he preferred comic books and video games to the great outdoors. It was curious that he'd have stumbled on a random cave in the middle of the forest.

Marcus stopped at the base of a hill. Lichen-covered boulders of various sizes surrounded the hill and climbed the side. He pointed between the largest of the two. "It's through there."

I stayed behind him and Lee, keeping close to Jennifer.

She'd been unusually quiet since Sarah's departure, and I could tell it was bothering her. She'd always been a bit shy, but never hesitated with a smile or a laugh. Here, in the middle of this too-quiet forest, everything felt off.

Together, we approached the mouth of the cave. It was barely taller than head height, ringed with ferns that hung down like teeth. It looked ready to devour us.

Lee laughed. "I'll be damned! I thought you were screwing with us! Maybe I can swipe some of my old man's smokes and bring them down here."

Jennifer tugged at my arm, reaching for my hand. I intertwined my fingers with hers, trying to keep the shit-eating grin off my face. "Should we go inside?" I asked.

"Hell yeah!" Lee shoved Marcus out of his way and walked to the mouth of the cave. "Damn, it's dark. Did anybody bring a flashlight?"

We all looked at Brandon expectantly, but he shook his head.

"We could always come back later with lights," Jennifer suggested.

I glanced down at her hand in mine. I wasn't about to pass up this chance. "Hey Lee, still got your lighter? It could help us get a look inside."

Lee grinned and reached in his pocket. He pulled out his lighter and flicked the flame to life. "Follow me."

Jennifer's grip on my hand tightened. "I don't think we should." Her troubled gaze met my eyes. "Something feels weird about this place."

I tugged her forward gently, making the plastic bangle

bracelets she wore clink together. "We might as well go ahead since we're here. You know Lee will just make us come back if we don't."

"Okay."

I sensed the uncertainty in her voice and glanced at Lee to make sure he was distracted. If he found out about my crush on Jennifer, I'd never hear the end of it. I leaned in close to her and whispered, "I'll stay with you the whole time, I swear."

"Holy shit, guys!" Lee had already gone in, holding the flame on his lighter a few seconds at a time before letting it die and sparking it back to life. Marcus and Brandon stood behind him, looking over his shoulder at something just out of my line of sight.

"W-what is it?" Jennifer asked.

"I don't know. A tree?" Marcus guessed as the flame flickered out again.

"Shut up, dipshit. Trees don't grow in caves. They need to photo...photo..." Lee flicked the lighter back to life.

"Photosynthesize," Brandon finished for him.

"It looks more like a statue," Jennifer said, straining to see from behind the others.

I stepped forward with false bravado. "Jennifer's right. It has a face..."

In the exact center of the cave stood the stump of some long-dead, petrified tree. Across the breadth of its ancient trunk, whether carved into it or formed by the peculiar whims of nature, there was the unmistakable likeness of a man's face.

"What's this?" Lee asked, and reached for a bit of string dangling from one of the branches.

Brandon had backed away and now stood just outside the cave. "This is messed up, dude. That looks like a person. Those look like arms!"

Lee stood frozen, his hand on the arm of the thing. A few seconds passed before he laughed, a nervous laugh I'd never heard from him before, and he lifted the string.

He must be afraid, I thought. I'd never seen Lee afraid.

Marcus inspected the strings and went pale. "It's Franklin's friendship bracelet."

"No..." Jennifer's voice was so low I was sure I'd been the only one to hear. She was trembling. I needed to get her out.

I looked at the others. "Why don't we come back when we have flashlights? That way we can get a better look at it?"

Lee was staring at the statue, tree stump, whatever *it* was. He turned on Marcus. "*You* put it here to try and scare us. Where did you find the carving, freak? Did you do it yourself? Been watching too much TV, and got bored? Decided to mess with us instead?" He shoved Marcus hard against the wall of the cave, his face inches away. "Well, I'm not buying it, creep." With each word he pressed a finger hard into Marcus's shoulder.

"Guys, come on," I said, trying to lower Lee's temperature a bit. "We should go find Sarah." In truth, I couldn't care less about Sarah, but I didn't know what else to say. Lee was a jerk, but there was no way I was going to get between him and Marcus.

CHAPTER 4

Yeah," I whispered to Jennifer. "The cave was real."

A waitress approached our table, notepad in hand. She must have been in her fifties, with a stained apron and a mustache shading her upper lip. She frowned at the napkin shreds strewn over the table. "Know what you'd like?"

I ordered a cheeseburger and fries. Jennifer asked for a slice of pumpkin pie. When the waitress walked away, Jennifer leaned across the table. "What was that thing inside? Was it...*Him*?"

There it was, the crazy part. The thing that had kept me from contacting her for the past twenty years. It was true that something had happened that summer, but we'd been kids. Just a bunch of kids. Too young to understand. Our minds had created a story, a boogeyman to blame instead. The difference was, I knew it wasn't real.

She interrupted my thoughts. "You heard the song too, right?" She sang the words, barely louder than a whisper:

*"Don't get lost along the way,
Forest Man is here to play..."*

My stomach knotted. "I heard you sing it." There was another memory of that song lingering in the back of my mind, one I wasn't ready to acknowledge yet.

The waitress returned with two glasses of water. Jennifer refused to meet my eyes.

"You never told me what *you* remember." I wasn't sure I wanted to know, but I needed to understand just how damaged she was.

Her gaze met mine. "Did I tell you I asked my parents about Franklin? I was so freaked out after we found his bracelet. I asked them what happened, why his family wasn't there."

I hadn't known. "What did they tell you?"

"Nothing. They wouldn't tell me anything. They said it wasn't my concern or some bullshit."

"It's no wonder you had such a hard time. We were kids, Jennifer. We wanted answers. If your parents refused to talk about it... if they didn't tell you the truth, then how were you supposed to know what to believe? How were you supposed to move on?" I reached across the table and took her hand in mine. I felt the same breathless rush I'd felt in the forest all those years ago.

"What truth?" she asked.

"That someone else was in the forest that summer. Someone besides us." I gave her hand a squeeze.

As I leaned forward, the label on the pill bottle came into focus. Xanax. The bottle said Xanax.

CHAPTER 5

The next morning, I returned to the Boulder Path. We hadn't agreed to meet or anything, I just felt drawn to it. I needed to go back to the cave and see if I could find evidence that it had all been a practical joke. Maybe then Jennifer would think I was a hero or something.

When I got to the path she was already standing there in her pink overall shorts, as if she'd been waiting for me. She grinned when she saw me. She was beautiful.

I held up my flashlight sheepishly. "I thought I'd go check it out."

She fiddled with the clasp of her overalls. "Me too. I…I mean, it was weird, right? That tree thing? The bracelet? You don't think Marcus would do that to scare us, do you?"

I shook my head. "Lee maybe, but not Marcus."

She nodded.

We entered the woods retracing our steps and left the path where Brandon's chalk marks began. I was grateful he'd left them. I could tell an oak from a maple and I knew bigger meant older when it came to trees, but that was where my knowledge ended. I was a child of the suburbs, not the forest.

I paused at the boulders leading to the cave's entrance. On each of the stones, a little higher than head height, were scratches that I might have mistaken as weathering if they had not been identical in size and shape. I stood on my tiptoes to look closer, and saw they were crude circular symbols carved into the stones. In the center of each circle were a pair of hands, woven together with what appeared to be vine. I had no idea what they were, or what they meant, but I had no doubt they were old.

"Jennifer, look."

"Were those here yesterday?" she asked.

"I didn't notice them, but maybe I was preoccupied." I blushed, remembering the feel of her hand in mine. "We should go in." At least inside, she wouldn't be able to see the redness of my cheeks.

We turned our flashlights on and entered the cave. I swept the beam to the center of the cave where the tree... thing...stood. It looked changed, somehow. I reached out to touch it, but Jennifer got there first.

Her flashlight clattered to the ground, breaking a silence I hadn't noticed until that moment. When she pulled her hand away it was covered in something red and sticky. She gasped, holding up a UFO-shaped key chain. "Marcus's?" she asked.

I studied the key chain dangling from her fingertips. We only knew one person who would own something like that. "Yeah. Do you think he left it here yesterday?"

She shook her head, looking down at her hands. "No. This...this wasn't here yesterday."

"Maybe he came back this morning?"

"I don't know, but something isn't right." She sniffed her hand and recoiled. "It smells like blood."

I shined my light along the cave's inner wall. It was covered with crimson words:

> *Take my hand and come with me*
> *Tweedle, deedle, deedle, dee*
> *I will follow where you go*
> *Tweedle deedle, deedle doe*
> *Don't get lost along the way*
> *Forest Man is here to play...*

The air in the cave was suddenly stifling. "That wasn't here yesterday, was it?" I stammered.

"No. It's all different. The cave changed."

"It must've been here. We probably missed it in the dark."

"No, Nate. This is fresh." The way she said it, using the word *fresh* instead of new, sent a chill up my spine.

There had to be a rational explanation. "Someone must have come back here. Maybe Lee. Right? Lee came back and did all this...to get back at Marcus for trying to scare him. Right?"

She stared, unblinking, at the words on the wall. The UFO key chain slid off her trembling fingers and fell to the ground at her feet.

I led her out of the cave and offered her my canteen.

"Here, wash that crap off." I couldn't bring myself to call it blood. Saying it out loud might make it true.

She moved mechanically. After her hands were clean, I led her back to the path, out of the forest.

When we returned to the lake, Sarah and Lee were standing on the white sand of the beach. Sarah's eyes were rimmed with tears. A discarded fishing pole lay at Lee's feet. It looked like they were arguing, and that they'd been at it for a while.

As we approached, Sarah turned away from Lee, walking forward to inspect Jennifer. "Where were you? I woke up this morning and you were already gone."

Jennifer stared at her feet, silent.

"We went back to the cave. It was...different today," I answered.

Lee flinched; the movement barely noticeable. "What do you mean, *different*?"

"There was something written on the walls...it looked like blood."

"The word 'blood' was written on the walls?"

"No. Something was written *on* the walls *in* blood."

"What was?"

"I don't know...it looked like a story, or a rhyme. Something about a man in the forest."

"Forest Man?" Lee asked.

"Yeah. That sounds right," I answered.

Lee muttered under his breath.

Jennifer's voice was barely above a whisper. "What does it mean?"

He shook his head. "It's bullshit, that's what. It's Marcus

being a freak. He should've let it go." He snatched up his fishing pole and stalked toward the cabins.

"Where are you going?" Sarah called after him.

"I'm going to pound that little jerk," he called back, vanishing down the road.

Sarah turned to Jennifer and me. "Is she okay?"

I squeezed Jennifer's hand. "I don't think she is. It was really creepy."

When Lee returned to the beach, Brandon was following him.

"Well, what happened?" I asked.

"He wasn't there," Lee answered.

Jennifer tensed and I placed a hand on her arm, then pressed Lee further. "What do you mean, 'wasn't there?'"

Lee sighed. I expected him to yell at me, but he just ran a hand through his hair.

Brandon broke the silence. "He was supposed to meet me this morning. We were going to break into Franklin's room to investigate a little and see if they left anything behind."

Sarah sat, propping her chin on her knees. "Supposed to?"

Brandon nodded. "Yeah, but he never showed up. I went to his place. I figured he overslept, or there was a *Twilight Zone* marathon on or something. But his parents said he was gone when they got up this morning."

Lee kicked the sand.

"So now what?" Sarah asked.

"We go to his house and wait for him," Lee answered. "He can't hide forever."

CHAPTER 6

Jennifer's hand trembled as she lifted her fork to her mouth. Her coffee mug was empty despite three refills, and I wondered whether it was the caffeine, the nerves, or the meds that gave her the shakes. She looked older than thirty-two, but the way she pushed her pie around on the plate before scooping up a bite made her seem younger. Had she always played with her food like that? Was it a habit she'd never grown out of? I wasn't sure.

I didn't know what I'd been expecting, contacting her after all these years. Well, maybe that wasn't entirely true; I'd thought if I saw her again that something would click. Either we'd hit it off and I could finally tell her how I felt, or nothing would happen and I could walk away laughing at how ridiculous I'd been by holding on to those feelings for so many years. The truth was, I needed to know how I felt about the person she'd become.

"Would you be willing to go back?" It was a dumb move, asking her to go back there, but maybe I could help her make peace with the past. If I took her back, and she saw there was nothing there, maybe she could move on. Maybe she'd want me to help her.

She didn't look surprised by my question. I wondered if she had suspected this. She'd probably known from the moment I messaged her that this was what I wanted, even before I knew myself.

"I think we should call Lee, too," she said.

I dropped the fry I'd been holding. I hadn't anticipated this. Of course, Lee had been with us all those years ago, but when I'd played the scenario out in my mind, it had always just been me and her who returned to the lake together. "Lee? I wouldn't even know how to get in touch with him."

She lifted her chin toward her phone. "I do."

My eyelid twitched. "You have his number?" All these years, she couldn't be bothered to keep in touch with me, but she had Lee's number programmed in her goddamned phone.

"Yeah. We dated for a while, if you could call it that. We were really just hooking up, I guess." She didn't meet my gaze, instead looking intently at her fingernails as she chipped away at the remaining black polish, flaking it onto the tabletop.

"Don't tell me." I didn't want to hear it. I didn't want to picture them together. Goddamn Lee. He must've taken advantage of her fragile mental state.

"He was pretty messed up about what happened that summer, too. I know he'll want to come with us." She pushed the polish flakes into a pile. I wondered why she wouldn't look at me.

The waitress returned and took Jennifer's empty plate, frowning at the mess on the table. I was glad for the interruption. It gave me a moment to think before I answered.

I did *not* want Lee to come. I knew this much, but I couldn't think of a good reason to tell her no. If I said no, I'd look like an asshole, and what if she liked the idea of going back, and went there alone with him instead? They might rekindle whatever had gone on between them. I couldn't risk it. "Fine. Call him. He can meet us there tomorrow, or not, but I'm not waiting for him."

What were the chances that he'd be able to drop everything and meet us by the cabins the next day?

The chances were pretty good, as it turned out.

CHAPTER 7

The Mathesons' cabin was one of the newer models, and was farther from the lake than the rest. What it lacked in location, it made up for in size. The newer cabins were at least twice the size of those closer to the lake. A large plastic swing set with a yellow tube slide sat untouched in the front yard.

Marcus's mom answered the door. A short, brunette woman in her late thirties, she was holding Aaron, Marcus's little brother, on her hip. "He told me he was going to meet you all this morning. You mean you kids haven't seen him at all today?"

I shook my head. "We thought he decided to stay home or something."

"He probably just wandered off looking for bugs or UFOs or something weird," Lee suggested. I resisted the urge to grind my heel into his toe.

"He does have his hobbies," Mrs. Matheson replied. "Have you kids had lunch? I can make you some pizza rolls and lemonade while you wait." She opened the door, allowing us inside.

"Thanks, that would be great," Sarah replied, taking Aaron from her. Sarah babysat for them during the summer for extra cash. According to Jennifer, they paid well.

Mrs. Matheson led us to the kitchen. We took seats around the table while she rummaged around in the fridge and the freezer, eventually popping a huge serving platter into the microwave. She placed a pitcher of iced lemonade in front of us, Kool-Aid packets, but with sliced lemons for garnish. When the microwave beeped, she put the steaming platter of pizza rolls and a stack of paper plates in the center of the table between us.

I kept an eye on Jennifer, hoping she'd snap out of her trance. She took a pizza roll, but instead of eating it, she tore it to pieces and left the shreds. I watched as orange grease puddled and stained her paper plate.

"Mrs. Matheson, could we ask you something?" Sarah rested her chin on her hand in a staged movement.

"What's on your mind, kids?" She watched Aaron chew cut up pieces of pizza roll from his booster seat. More of the roll ended up smeared on the tablecloth than in his mouth.

"Marcus said that Franklin went missing last year here, at the lake," Sarah began. "He said you were all still here when it happened."

Mrs. Matheson looked around the table. She must've been wondering how much she should tell us. Finally, she sighed. "It was a terrible thing, really."

"So, it's true?" Sarah asked, eyes shining.

"Yes. Franklin disappeared, and the police did a search of the area. I'm afraid I can't tell you much more than that. We left soon after he went missing because Marcus had gotten very sick. He was sleepwalking and mumbling. He ran a high fever, too."

I took the last roll from the plate, wiping my greasy hands on my jeans. "What was wrong with him?"

Mrs. Matheson took the empty platter from the table and transferred it to the sink. "The doctors said it was stress. I didn't even want to come back this year, but he begged. He said it would do him good to see his lake friends. Don't tell him I told you, but I want you all to watch out for him. I know he's... odd. Be kind."

"We'll look out for him, Mrs. Matheson Don't worry," I said before swallowing down the last of my lemonade.

Lee nodded. "Could we leave a note for him in his room?"

"Sure! He'd like that."

Sarah lifted the empty pitcher from the table. "You guys go ahead. I'll help clean up."

Marcus's room was exactly as I remembered it. Large red bunk beds lined one wall in case any of us stayed over. He'd used his sleeping bag and blankets to make one of the bottom bunks into a fort. On top of his desk was a Nintendo and a stack of games. I felt a stab of jealousy; I'd begged my parents to buy me one for months with no success. I couldn't believe he had one at the lake.

Nothing was out of place that I could tell. All of his things were still there, right down to the Ninja Turtles duffle bag lying in the corner. Wherever he'd gone, he hadn't taken anything with him.

"Look around," Lee ordered. "See if you find anything useful, or any clues to where he might have gone."

While Brandon searched the bookshelf, Lee paced, muttering to himself. He stopped in front of the desk. I watched as he lifted a notebook and flipped through the pages. He cast a surreptitious glance around the room before rolling it up and sticking it in his back pocket. I was surprised the notebook was the only thing he swiped.

I took Jennifer's hand, a gesture that was becoming more natural each time. "C'mon, we'll check over here."

I opened the closet door and pushed the clothes aside. Jennifer made a strangled sound in the back of her throat. I saw a flash of red, and immediately pushed the clothes back, but I wasn't fast enough. She'd already seen the writing.

Lee and Brandon rushed over. Behind the clothes in the closet, in crimson letters, was the rhyme: *Don't get lost along the way, Forest Man is here to play.*

Lee kicked the closet door. "He's somewhere. And when I find him, I'm going to pound him." He stormed out of the room, and we fell in line behind him.

We spent the rest of the afternoon at the beach. The sun beat down from overhead, reflecting off the sand and making the temperature miserable. We were all on edge. None of us mentioned Marcus. No one said much of anything. Lee and Brandon cast line after line into the lake, catching nothing. Sarah spread out on a beach towel with a Nancy Drew novel in hand. I tried to get Jennifer interested in building a sand castle. She pushed mounds of sand around with her hands, but mostly just watched.

At sunset Mrs. Matheson walked down to the beach. "Have you kids seen Marcus? He never came home."

Lee flinched. Brandon placed a hand on his shoulder. "No Ma'am. We haven't seen him."

"You're sure?"

"Yeah," Brandon answered.

"When was the last time you all saw him?" she asked.

"Yesterday," Lee said through clenched teeth.

She turned back down the road towards the cabins, her face a mask of concern.

Sarah looked up from her book. "What was that about?"

Brandon threw down his fishing pole. "You know what! Marcus is gone, just like Franklin, and it has something to do with that cave."

"Don't talk crazy." Lee's face twisted with rage. "It means that Marcus is trying to scare us. That's all. Just think about it; he tells us about Franklin, and then just happens to mention that freaky cave? Nuh-uh, he's messing with us."

Brandon shook his head. "Marcus wouldn't do that. He might be weird, but he isn't mean. He'd be afraid to be out by himself for this long, especially after dark. What if something's there? What if there's someone in the woods? We need to tell our folks."

Lee swung hard, and we all heard the sickening thud of his fist against Brandon's face. "We aren't telling anyone! Do you understand? We don't talk about the cave, or the woods. Nothing. And if I find out that you did, I'll kill you!"

"Jesus, Lee! Chill out," Sarah said. "He won't say anything." She bent down to check on Brandon, who was cradling his cheek. "You don't have to act like a freaking barbarian."

"I don't need this right now." Lee scooped up his battered fishing rod and headed down the road toward his cabin.

CHAPTER 8

ennifer went outside to call Lee while I paid the check. I left the diner and spotted her on the corner, lighting up a cigarette. The flames illuminated her face, reminding me of that night at the bonfire. I could see hints of the girl she had been beneath the lines on her face.

"Well?" I asked.

"He'll be there. Said it was about time we decided to go back."

I winced. Lee had been there for her, kept in touch with her, and I'd run away like a fucking coward. Maybe if I had been there, things would have turned out differently for her. "Jennifer, I'm sorry I didn't do a better job of keeping in touch. I just..."

She shrugged. "It didn't touch you and Brandon, not like me and Lee. You didn't understand."

"I understood well enough. I just didn't know what to say to you." In the nearly empty parking lot, my Subaru sat beneath a blinking security light. I didn't see her car anywhere. I wondered how she'd gotten there.

She took a long drag from her cigarette. "You don't have to live with the guilt, Nate. I was given a choice, and I made a bad one. That decision, the guilt... it's haunted me since that summer."

"What do you mean, you were given a choice? Brandon told the police, and they didn't find anything. What else could you have done?"

She tossed her cigarette on the ground and stamped it out. "I don't mean the police. I mean *Him. He* gave me a choice, and I told Him to take Sarah."

I stared at her. I wondered if she'd had one too many Xanax, or one too many therapy sessions. I wondered what her parents had told her, what her therapists had told her, and what stories she had told herself to make sense of what happened. After years of torturing myself, I'd finally decided that Forest Man was just a story, one we'd invented in our subconscious minds because the truth was too frightening to confront. There was someone in the woods when we were kids, and it was that person who had taken our friends.

"If we're inviting Lee, shouldn't we call Brandon, too?" I asked, ready to change the subject.

Jennifer shook her head. "No. Lee never forgave him for all that shit with the police. He thought Brandon was trying to blame him for what happened to Marcus."

"I don't give a good goddamn what Lee thinks. We're going to ask Brandon to come too. He was there. He's a part of this whether Lee likes it or not."

She flicked another smoke from her packet and lit it up. "I don't know him anymore."

I held up my keys. "I know how to find him." I'd looked him up on the internet once, just like I had with the others. I'd driven by his house a hundred times, always wondering which would be the time I'd stop the car and knock on his door. I'd almost worked up the courage once, but when his two-story brick house with the perfect white fence out front came into view, I saw his two daughters out playing in the yard, and I couldn't bring myself to darken his door with long forgotten memories.

Tonight was different, though. Jennifer needed me.

She climbed into the passenger seat of my Subaru and switched on the radio. She flipped from station to station, never stopping for more than a moment as I pulled out of the diner's parking lot and through Talvot Square, heading toward the nicer side of town. The side where the wealthier residents lived. It seemed strange to me that after all these years, we'd each moved closer to Lake Swart, as if something about it just couldn't let us go.

In the close quarters of the car, I detected the faint scent of floral perfume beneath the stench of cigarette smoke. Together, the combination of scents was nauseating, but she'd worn perfume to meet me, and maybe that meant something.

She exhaled a whistle, taking in the sight of the house as I pulled the car into Brandon's driveway and shut off the ignition. "Damn, this is nice."

It was late, and the porch light was off, but stake lights illuminated the walkway leading to the porch. "Wait here," I said to Jennifer as I exited the car.

I climbed the stairs and stood on the front stoop trying to figure out what I was going to say before I pressed the doorbell. Or maybe I should knock?

The door swung open in the midst of my internal debate. Brandon stood before me, aged, but essentially the same. He wore Old Navy pajamas; the kind where the tops and bottoms were a matching set. They seemed oddly appropriate for the person I imagined him to be. My tongue fumbled for the words I wanted to say.

"Who are you, and what do you want? Don't you know it's 1:00 am? Are you having car trouble or something?" He looked right at me, but there was no sign of recognition on his face.

"No, Brandon. It's me, Nate." I saw the look on his face when he realized what that meant. When all the memories came flooding back. He aged ten years in a single moment.

"Nate." My name sounded like a bad taste in his mouth. He pulled the door open a little wider. "Do you want to come in?"

Relief washed over his features as I shook my head no. "Jennifer's waiting for me in the car."

He looked past me, but I doubted he could see much in the dark. "You didn't come here at one in the morning to chit chat about old times. What do you want?" he asked, crossing his arms over his chest.

"We're going back," I answered.

"To Lake Swart? You have got to be out of your goddamn mind." Maybe he was right. It was crazy to come here. I was certain that Brandon and his perfect house and matching pajamas would want no part in what I was planning.

"Honey, who is it?" A woman's voice came from behind him, inside the house.

He glanced over his shoulder. "No one, sweetheart. Just someone lost who stopped for directions."

"At one in the morning? I thought everyone had GPS," the voice replied.

"Please," I whispered. "If not for me, do it for Jennifer. After what she lost, we owe her this at least."

"Fine, but you've got to leave. Now."

The door closed before I'd even turned to walk back to the car.

Jennifer had her feet propped on the dashboard. She'd finally settled on a radio station blasting some pop song I didn't know.

"He's in," I said, slipping into the driver's seat.

She nodded. "You got any booze at your place?"

I thought about her bottle of Xanax and wondered if it was a good idea, but she placed her hand on my thigh, and all my good intentions disappeared. I turned the key, bringing the car to life and turned off on the street, headed back across town, towards my apartment.

CHAPTER 9

The morning after Marcus had disappeared, the lake community was crawling with police cars and flashing lights. He hadn't come home, not that any of us expected him to. Not even Lee, despite all of his bluster the night before.

My parents sat me down and explained that they expected me to cooperate with the police. I thought about telling them that Lee had punched Brandon, and that he'd forbidden us from talking, but what would I say? That there was a creepy statue in a cave, and we think it might have come to life and taken our friend?

I excused myself as soon as I could and headed to Jennifer's cabin. I hoped a night's rest had helped her recover, but I worried what her reaction would be now that Marcus was officially missing. She'd need me to be there for her.

Sarah met me at the door.

"Where is she?" I asked.

Sarah rolled her eyes. "Well, hello to you, too."

"I'm sorry, Sarah. It's just...after yesterday, you know, I was worried about her." I could feel all six shades of red my face had turned.

"I don't know where she is. She's been acting weird since yesterday." She didn't bother masking the annoyance in her tone.

I clenched my fists at my side. "One of our friends is missing, and you just let her go off alone?"

She kicked a pebble across the porch. "It isn't like she told me she was leaving. She just got up and left without saying anything. I think she took my book with her."

"Thanks," I called over my shoulder, heading toward the Boulder Path. If she wasn't missing, I had a hunch where she'd be.

I left the path at the usual spot and found Jennifer sitting just inside the cave, right in front of...*Him*. I don't know when I had come to think of the tree stump as a *him*, but it felt right. The forest surrounding the mouth of the cave had somehow grown thicker, trying to conceal its dark secrets. The ferns fringing the top had grown larger and hung down from the top of the opening, like the teeth of some ancient beast, ready to feed. It was the same cave, and yet it was changed.

Jennifer sang in a low voice. "*Take my hand and come with me, tweedle, deedle, deedle, dee...*"

"Jennifer?" I placed a hand on her shoulder. She jumped. "What are you doing out here?"

When she turned, I noticed she still wore her pajamas, and was weirdly barefooted. Her feet were covered in dried mud and angry red cuts.

"He wants to play."

"Who?"

"The Forest Man. He's lonely, and He wants us to come play with Him."

I crouched down beside her. "Who's the Forest Man, Jennifer?"

"*I will follow where you go, tweedle deedle, deedle doe...*"

I grabbed her by the shoulders and gently shook her. "Jennifer?"

"Marcus sent Franklin to play. Lee sent Marcus to play. Now, it's my turn." She was speaking gibberish.

"Come on, we're getting out of here." I draped her arm over my shoulder and hoisted her up, dragging her away from the cave. "We're going to go back and talk to the police, okay? We're going to tell them everything. Screw Lee."

"No." Her voice was husky and low. "No, you can't tell the police. Promise you won't."

"This is serious. Something is happening, and we need to tell the grownups."

Tears streaked the dirt on her face. "Please, please promise you won't."

It was her eyes that convinced me. Snot and drool dribbled down her chin, but her eyes shined with...fear? I wasn't sure. "Okay, I promise."

I turned for one last glimpse at the cave, and saw Sarah's book propped against the tree stump. I half-led, half-carried Jennifer back to the lake.

By the time we emerged from the forest, her parents had noticed her missing and panicked, fearing the worst. Her mother, a tall blonde wearing a sunhat and a pair of Ray-Bans, gave a nervous laugh and patted my shoulder. "Thank you for bringing her back, Nate. I'm sure she's just worried about Marcus. I mean, we all are."

I nodded. There was nothing else to say. I wanted to tell them about the song, the book, and those crazy things she'd said to me about the Forest Man, but when I looked at Jennifer I just couldn't. I had promised. It would've been a betrayal.

My parents called me back home, so I went inside our cabin and waited. My dad tried to interest me in a game of chess, but by the third time I'd moved my knight the wrong way, he'd gotten annoyed and stopped trying.

"Why do I have to stay here anyway? Why can't I meet up with the others?" I asked, staring absently at the abandoned game pieces. I was sure that by being cooped up with my parents I was missing all the excitement.

Mom sighed. "Because the police are searching the woods. They can't have you kids walking through a crime scene."

"A crime scene? They think it was a crime?"

Dad gave her a warning look. "Something happened. We don't know what. It's too soon to jump to any conclusions, so just let the police do their job."

"What are they looking for?" I asked.

"Your friend Brandon took them into the woods. He said he knew somewhere they should check."

My heart felt like it would pound right out of my chest. Of course Brandon would.

CHAPTER 10

I pushed open the door of my apartment, regretting that I hadn't bothered cleaning up the dirty laundry strewn over the furniture, or the empty bottles on the coffee table.

Jennifer stepped inside, giving the place a once-over. If the mess bothered her, she didn't give any indication. She turned on me with those eyes that dripped sadness and need. "What's a girl gotta do to get a drink around here?" She grinned, but it seemed halfhearted. I wondered if that was how everything was with her now, if every experience was laced with some sort of lingering melancholy.

I walked over to my liquor cabinet. Again, I wondered if she should be drinking. Was it safe to mix alcohol with her medications? I could ask, but she was a grown woman, capable of making her own decisions, wasn't she? Besides, I could hardly blame her. Tonight had resurrected memories I'd left back in that forest long ago, but for her, it was a reminder of all the things that had followed her home. I grabbed a bottle of Jack by the neck. "You like Whiskey Sours?"

"I like whatever you can make." She didn't bother moving yesterday's shirt from the back of the ratty gray couch before settling in and making herself at home.

I went into the kitchen to fill up an ice bucket. I hadn't expected this turn of events. Jennifer was in my apartment, on my couch. I took a deep breath. It wasn't a big deal. I'd dated other women. I'd slept with other women. This night was just like any other. Except that it wasn't, and I wasn't fooling myself. I tucked the ice bucket under my arm and went back into the living room, where she waited.

The bottle was slippery in my hand from the sweat on my palms. I sat two glasses on the coffee table and mixed the drinks, going a little heavier on the booze than if I'd been drinking alone. She patted the cushion beside her, and I sat.

"So, what have you been doing with yourself all these years, Nate?" She tipped up her glass, taking a long swallow.

"I... uh... I teach over at Union Grove." I sloshed the liquid around in my glass, watching the maraschino cherry circle the ice cubes. I was afraid I'd blush if I looked her in the eye.

"Okay, Professor. What do you teach?" She turned up the glass again, this time leaving it nearly empty.

"History."

She cocked her head, raised an eyebrow, but said nothing.

My gaze dropped back to my drink. I'd never felt embarrassed about my job before, like it wasn't enough. Why did I now? It seemed absurd to me.

"Nice," she answered and rattled the ice in her glass. I took her cue and walked over to the liquor cabinet. This time I returned with the bottle.

"What about you?" I asked, offering it to her.

She took it from me and topped up her glass. All whiskey, she didn't bother with the sour this time. "I worked at the last Blockbuster in town. They held on until 2010."

"Longer than most." My eyes swept over her torn jeans and black Converse.

"Yeah. After they closed down, I bounced between a few jobs." She took another long sip.

"And now?"

She frowned at her glass. "I've been out of work for about three months."

"Oh." I lifted my glass to my lips, but didn't take a drink. She'd eventually need to get home, wherever that was, and I'd need to be sober enough to drive her.

"I know what you're thinking, but it wasn't my fault." She turned up her glass again. I hadn't seen anyone drink so much so fast since college.

"Hey, I wasn't thinking anything." I placed my hand on her knee and hoped the gesture was comforting rather than creepy. "I knew you when we were kids. You were always amazing. We all go through rough patches."

She smiled and refilled her glass again. At this rate, I was going to need another bottle.

CHAPTER 11

At the lake, we all held a collective breath while Officer Hollis, a man with a square jaw and crew cut, opened the door to Marcus's closet.

The bloodstained words that had terrified us were gone.

He leaned a hand on the doorframe, glaring down at us. He looked exhausted, and not at all amused. "This is the closet you meant, right?"

He was giving us a chance, I knew, but I couldn't stop myself. "It was here!"

Brandon nodded grimly. "It's gone. Just like the cave."

"Kids," Officer Hollis said. "Caves and words don't just up and vanish."

"But they were there!" Brandon insisted.

"This isn't some game, son! We were in those woods all afternoon while you led us on a wild goose chase, and now this nonsense?" He slammed his hand against the wall.

There was no way we were going to convince him we were telling the truth.

"Come on, guys," I said. "Let's go."

A few minutes later, we all sat on the couch while Mr. Matheson reamed us out about lying to the police.

"You kids know better. Every bit of time and attention you take away from these officers puts Marcus in more danger. You should all be ashamed of yourselves!"

I saw Lee pinch the inside of Brandon's leg. Brandon squirmed, but didn't make a sound.

It'd been Brandon who decided to tell the police everything. When he took them to the Boulder Path to find the cave, they'd circled the path for hours. He couldn't find his chalk marks and they couldn't find the cave. The police finally decided he was lying to them. When we left the Matheson house that evening, we were instructed to go straight to our cabins.

Brandon pulled me aside as we left. "Dude. Something seriously weird is going on."

"I know," I answered. I knew he was talking about more than just Jennifer, but I could think of little else. "Jennifer's not okay, and I don't know what to do."

"I have an idea," Brandon said.

I stopped and turned to face him. "It's about time someone did. Let's get the others."

"No." He held his compass in his hand, running his thumb over the surface. "Lee's being a shit, Jennifer's lost her mind, and Sarah's too prissy to be useful. It's got to be me and you."

"Okay." I glanced back down the main road. The others were headed toward their cabins. It was strange for everyone to be so quiet. "What did you have in mind?"

Brandon motioned for me to follow. We walked in knee-high weeds along the edge of the street until we arrived at the cabin belonging to Franklin's family. He led me around the side yard where we wouldn't be visible from the main road, then looked around, as if he suspected someone might be eavesdropping. Seeing nothing, he leaned in close. "The whole cave was gone. I don't know how or why. I couldn't find it."

"Do you think it disappeared?" Under normal circumstances, it might've seemed like a stupid question, but circumstances were anything but normal.

Brandon shook his head. "I doubt it. I don't know what happened, but I think we should go back there."

"Say we go back and find it again. Then what? You already tried to tell the grownups about it, and now they don't believe us. We can't prove anything." It felt strange to actually talk about it. As if that made it more real, somehow. So far, even among ourselves, we hadn't said much. Partly from Lee's intimidation, and partly, I think, just from plain old fear.

Brandon led me around the cabin to a small tool shed in the back. "We've got to destroy it." He lifted the padlock on the shed's door, turning it over and studying the locking mechanism. "Keep a lookout."

My hands began to tremble as I realized that he meant to break open the shed. I'd never committed a crime before. But since no one lived there anymore, maybe it wasn't a *real* crime. "Can you pick it?"

He retrieved a Swiss Army Knife from one of his many

pockets and used it to pry the latch away from the wood, rendering the padlock useless.

"Whoa, neat!"

"Shhh!"

My face burned hot. "Sorry," I whispered.

He pushed open the door and turned on his penlight, sweeping its tiny beam across the shed's interior. The light glinted off something hanging on the wall, and Brandon stepped inside, not waiting to see whether I followed.

He walked to the farthest side of the shed and lifted a hatchet hanging from a peg, offering me the handle.

"What am I supposed to do with this?" I asked.

"We're gonna make kindling out of that sucker."

I threaded the hatchet's handle through a belt loop. "Do you think if we destroy it, we'll get Franklin and Marcus back?"

"I don't know," he replied, sending the beam over the wall again, "but, it might break whatever trance Jennifer's in."

My heart gave one hard pound, then another. He was right. If we destroyed the stump-thing, maybe she'd go back to normal again.

"Let's go then."

This time I led the way as we stumbled out of the shed, and back onto the Boulder Path.

CHAPTER 12

The whiskey was gone, and along with it, the better part of a bottle of rum. Jennifer leaned forward and placed her hand on my knee. She meant the gesture to be intimate as far as I could tell, but she was off balance, and over-enunciated her words. "What are you really trying to do?"

She must've thought I was trying to get her drunk. But I didn't pour all those drinks, she did. "What do you mean?"

"Going back to Lake Swart? Like, why now? It's been twenty years." Her words slurred despite the fact that she spoke as if each one required intense concentration.

I scanned the room until my eyes fell on the rum bottle. How much of this conversation would she actually remember? I might as well tell her the truth. "After all these years, I haven't stopped thinking about that summer. I haven't stopped thinking about you, either. I wanted to see you. To see how you were doing."

Her expression softened as she did the mental calculus. "You want to go back... for me?"

It was heartbreaking how surprised she sounded, as though she couldn't believe someone would want to do something like that for her. "Well, yeah." It wasn't articulate, but I didn't trust my own words.

She scooted closer and pressed her lips to mine. She tasted like cigarettes and booze. When I was twelve, I used to imagine what kissing her would be like. In my dreams, she'd always tasted of cherries and vanilla, and her kiss was a sweet, tentative thing. In reality, it was a drunken, sloppy kiss born of too much alcohol and God-knows-what-all medications.

I pulled away. "I should go freshen up." I could've kicked myself. Of all the cheesy, cliched lines to come up with... freshen up? Like I was a 1960s housewife.

Jennifer didn't seem to notice. She sunk back into the couch, undoing the top button of her shirt. "Don't take too long..." She missed the second button and giggled, taking it between her clumsy fingers.

I locked the bathroom door behind me and turned on the tap. The cold water felt good against the heat of my face. If I slept with her, would I be taking advantage? If I said no, would she think I was rejecting her, and be offended? I had no idea; all of my concentration was focused on the pressure against my zipper.

I paced in front of the mirror. What was the worst that could happen? The awkward morning-after conversation? Or worse, what if she just left in the morning without saying anything? I'd driven her here, but she could probably call an Uber or something. What if she didn't remember, and assumed I'd taken advantage?

I placed my hands on either side of the sink and looked at my reflection in the mirror. I loved this girl once. I would not do anything to disgrace that.

I inhaled a deep breath and headed back to the living room.

Jennifer lay slumped on the couch, snoring gently. Her shirt was off, exposing a black bra with pink polka dots. She didn't stir as I wrapped my arms beneath her and carried her to bed. Sleep had erased the traces of worry and anxiety from her face that I'd already begun to associate with this new, older version of her.

I pulled the blanket around her shoulders and kissed her forehead, closing the door behind me as I went to make myself comfortable on the couch.

I dreamed of Lake Swart, missing friends, and something tucked away in a cave, waiting for us. I wondered if it would still be there when we went back.

CHAPTER 13

Rain clouds threatened the horizon. Brandon moved slowly, scanning the forest as we walked, waiting to see if the cave would reveal itself to us this time.

When we finally reached the chalk-marked trees, the thunder rolled low in the distance, followed by a fine drizzle. Clouds of mist rose where rain fell against rock, giving the woods a preternatural appearance.

Brandon stared at the chalk marks, dumbfounded. "Dude, I swear they weren't here before."

"I believe you."

He lifted his hat and scratched the top of his head. "I don't understand. I must've gotten lost or mixed up."

"Maybe it's magic or something?" I suggested.

"Don't be a baby, Nate. Magic isn't real."

His eye was still swollen and bruised courtesy of Lee's fist, so I resisted the urge to shove him. "Two of our friends are gone, another is cata... cata—"

"Catatonic?" he offered.

"Catatonic. Not to mention the cave doesn't exist when grownups are around. It's like it wants *us* to find it. You know you didn't get lost. You've never been lost!"

A streak of lightning flashed through the sky followed by a crack of thunder and the rain fell in earnest. "Let's go," Brandon said, heading in the direction of the cave.

The storm rendered the sky blurry and vague. We twisted our way through the lichen-covered rocks, running for the shelter of the cave. Creepy or not, at least the inside would be dry, and we had work to do. I slipped and stumbled over roots and vines, trying to keep Brandon's pace.

We skidded to a stop at the cave's yawning entrance. The muted sunlight from the stormy skies made the interior darker and more foreboding than I remembered. My hands cramped from clutching the hatchet.

Brandon peered into the cave as though it were the first time he'd seen it.

"Come on, man. We've got to go in." I held the hatchet out in front of me, brandishing it like a weapon on our approach.

"Wait." Rivulets of rain steamed down his face. He searched his pockets and pulled out his pen light. "We aren't going in without this." He clicked it on, and I followed him inside.

The cave's interior smelled sharp and metallic. The walls were still coated in red. A thunderous boom outside was followed by a brilliant flash. "Holy shit!" I screamed and scrambled farther into the darkness. My heart pounded with a panicked rhythm in my chest. I was glad it was

Brandon here and not Lee. He'd have never let me live down that scream.

Brandon swept the beam around, letting it rest on the tree trunk thing. His trembling hands caused the light to vibrate. "You still got the hatchet?" he asked. He knew I did, but his words made me realize he meant for *me* to destroy it. His eyes darted from the stump to the walls of the cave.

Red ooze leaked from the top of the stump, dripping down the sides like some strange and slowly seeping volcano. Sarah's book still lay propped against it, now covered in red. The world felt still for a moment as though this monstrosity, pulsating with life, had been waiting for our arrival. I held the hatchet out to Brandon, shaking my head. "Nu-uh. This was your idea."

He didn't respond.

We were all afraid of whatever was in the cave, even Lee despite his talk, but facing it again, something inside Brandon snapped. It might have been the changes in the cave since the last time he'd been there, or the substance that now covered the stump, but I was fairly certain it was the creeping realization he hadn't been lost when he came looking before. He hadn't found the cave because this thing inside hadn't wanted him to.

The light sent flickering shadows across the cave's wall. A low rumble came from somewhere deeper within the cave.

"Did you hear that?" I asked.

He nodded.

"What was it?"

"Echoes. Echoes from the thunderstorm." His voice quavered.

I hefted the hatchet, stepping towards the stump. There was no use delaying, and one look at Brandon told me he wouldn't do it. He couldn't.

I swung, and the hatchet's blade sparked against the stump as if I'd hit flint on steel. The sparks lit the cave enough for me to see Brandon still frozen behind me.

The wind picked up, howling, and sending a spray of water inside the cave. I raised the blade again and struck the stump. A concussive boom thundered outside. I looked up in enough time to see a dazzling flash, and the silhouette of a group of children standing at the cave's mouth, hand in hand.

I shouted with surprise and stumbled. The sound and motion shook Brandon free of his stupor. "What?" He swept the tiny beam of light across the cave.

"Someone was there!" I gestured frantically toward the entrance, but even I could see there was nothing there now.

"Was it Lee?" Brandon asked. "Maybe he followed us." He didn't sound convinced.

"No. It was something else—"

Another sound came from behind us. It wasn't the howling of the wind or echoes from the storm. It was laughter, but not the kind born of joy or happiness. It was sharp and cruel, and as it echoed in the chamber around us, I recognized the sound of the voice.

Brandon and I turned towards the sound at the same time. He slowly swept the light over red walls stretching back so far that the darkness couldn't be penetrated. As he ran the beam over the right side of the cave, a white oval came into view.

Not just an oval. A face.

Marcus's skin was maggoty-white. One eye was open, the other was crushed and dangling from its socket by the optic nerve. His bloated body made him seem larger than he was; his features twisted into a sneer he'd never worn in life. He reached a hand towards me with dirty, blackened claws.

Brandon dropped the light and we ran out of the cave. As we made our way through the forest, Marcus's voice sang out behind us. *"Don't get lost along the way. Forest Man is here to play..."*

CHAPTER 14

It took a moment to register that the pounding noise was coming from my front door. I grabbed my phone from the coffee table and lit it up: 6:45 am. "I'm coming," I grumbled, stretching my back. The couch had never made for comfortable sleeping.

I ran a hand through my hair and tried to brush the wrinkles out of my shirt. The banging grew more insistent.

I jerked the door open. Brandon stood there with a bulging folder tucked under his left arm. "Good. You're home," he said, brushing past me into the living room.

My thoughts were slow and clumsy from sleep. I watched dumbfounded as he opened the folder and pulled out a stack of printed papers, spreading them out across my coffee table. "How do you know where I live?" I asked.

"You aren't the only one who knows how to use a search engine," he replied, not looking up.

"Why are you here at the ass crack of dawn?"

"The same reason you were at my house at 1:00 am.

When I saw you, I started remembering things I hadn't thought about in a long time, so I started digging. I did some research on Lake Swart."

I rubbed the crust of sleep from my eyes. "So, you're here to give me a book report?"

"You're the one that came to me, wise ass. You asked me to come. You don't want my help? Fine." He grabbed the nearest papers and started stacking them.

"No, no. I'm sorry. It's just... I didn't have enough sleep. Why don't I go put on some coffee, and you can show me what you found, all right?"

He nodded and laid the papers back down on the table.

I stumbled into the kitchen, grabbing a filter and a scoop from the cabinet. I measured out the maximum amount my old-fashioned drip maker would hold and hit the start button.

I pulled out three mugs and poured sugar into a chipped blue dish that hadn't been used in years. I opened the fridge and reached for the carton of milk and a box of leftover donuts I was pretty sure had gone stale.

The coffee maker grumbled and sputtered out the last of the hot liquid, and I loaded everything onto a tray and carried it to the living room.

Jennifer sat on the couch beside Brandon, wearing one of my long-sleeved shirts. Black lines of mascara smeared beneath her eyes. It was weird seeing the two of them sitting there together, so different than they had been, but so familiar to me. It was almost as if we picked up where we'd left off, and nothing had changed.

I cleared my throat and they both looked up.

Jennifer's eyes lit. "Coffee? You're an angel."

I balanced the tray carefully in my arms as I crossed the room. I filled a mug for myself, steaming black, and rummaged in the box for a glazed donut. "So, what's with the papers?"

Jennifer joined me and filled her own mug. There was a lightness in her step that hadn't been there yesterday. No hangover, which was shocking considering how much she'd imbibed. I wondered what she remembered from last night. There would be a time to ask those questions, but it wasn't now.

I looked down at the mess on the table. "Milk and sugar?" I asked in Brandon's direction.

He grunted. I wasn't sure what that meant, so I brought it to him black.

He nodded his thanks and sat the cup on the table. "Weird shit has been happening at Lake Swart for a long time. Even before it got turned into a summer lake community, there were reports of people going missing. Mostly children. Back then it wasn't Lake Swart. It was Noccalula Lake. The development company renamed it when they built the cabins."

I sipped my coffee, willing the caffeine into my bloodstream. "You don't honestly mean to tell me that you believe this Forest Man bullshit, do you?"

Brandon's eyes met mine. I could feel the weight of his judgement as he held my gaze. "You don't remember seeing Marcus's body in the cave?"

My heart sank. I'd hoped Brandon would be my ally. The one other person from that summer who knew Forest Man wasn't real, and that there was a rational explanation for the things we thought we'd seen. As an adult, he'd seemed the most well-adjusted. He had a good job and a family.

I swallowed a scalding mouthful of coffee to push donut crumbs down my throat. "No." Even as I said it, flashes of memory crept into the corner of my mind. The cave. A storm. A hatchet.

Jennifer sat her mug down hard on the table. "Why didn't you tell me, Nate?" I couldn't tell from her tone if she was hurt or just angry.

"Because it wasn't real. We went to the cave to destroy the thing. We were terrified and we psyched each other up. The thunder and lightning had us on edge and we imagined things. Even if it *was* real, someone had probably just stashed his body there and our imaginations did the rest." I took another sip to keep myself from saying more.

"The cave was different when we went back," Brandon said. "Changed. How do you explain that?"

"Whoever was lurking in the woods that summer was probably camping out there," I suggested.

"I don't think campers usually paint verses on cave walls in blood."

"First off," I swallowed another dry hunk of donut, "we don't know for sure that it was blood. And secondly, whoever was out there may have seen us poking around and decided to fuck with us and scare us off."

Jennifer brushed a strand of stray hair from her forehead. "But why didn't you—"

Brandon held up a hand and cut off her question. "It doesn't matter. If he doesn't remember, he doesn't remember. But I'm telling you, this stuff has been going on since before Franklin."

"What do you mean?" Jennifer asked, taking her seat beside him on the couch.

Brandon sat back on the couch and took a drink. He winced and frowned at the mug. "Got sugar?"

"Yeah." I nodded toward the tray. When he got up to fix his coffee, I took his place beside Jennifer.

Brandon shoveled two heaping spoonfuls of sugar into his mug. The spoon clanked against the side of the cup as he stirred.

I scooted closer to Jennifer, aware that Brandon was watching from across the room.

He took a long swallow and joined us by the table, shuffling through and picking out several papers, sliding them towards me. "Nineteen sixty-four, a Boy Scout troop went camping in the woods near the lake. Three Scout leaders and twelve boys went on the trip. Only two made it back.

"Nineteen seventy-eight, three college students decided to go swimming at the lake. The official report said they'd likely drowned, but no bodies were ever found. They vanished. Just like Franklin, Marcus, and Sarah."

At the mention of Sarah, I turned to Jennifer. Her eyes were closed, as if that somehow lessened the burden of hearing it again.

"Those could be accidents," I said. "College students get drunk and drown. Even Boy Scouts get lost. You did, remember?" It was a low blow, but he'd asked for it when he brought up Sarah.

His eyes narrowed. "You know I wasn't lost. You admitted it yourself back there in the cave."

"Yeah, when I was twelve years old and all these stories had me scared shitless!" I slammed my mug down and coffee splashed over the sides and onto the papers collected near the edge.

"Nineteen eighty-three," Brandon continued as though the interruption hadn't happened, "a pair of hikers went missing in the area."

I shrugged. "Hikers get lost, too."

"Developers bought the land in the nineties, built the community, and renamed the lake. Shortly after that is when our families would've started buying the properties. You obviously know what happened when we were there, but that wasn't the end of it. When we all stopped going after that summer, there were other families and other disappearances." He pushed a few of the coffee-stained papers towards me.

Jennifer exhaled a low whistle. "How long have you been researching this?"

"All night."

"Only one night, and you've already found all of this stuff?" She was sifting through the papers he'd pushed towards us.

I felt a pang of jealousy. If Brandon could do this much

research with only an internet connection, I could've done much more using the library at Union Grove. I'd never bothered looking into it because I hadn't believed any of it was real. But Brandon believed in something, and my plans were quickly going to hell. "Hey, man, will you help me take this stuff back to the kitchen?"

He nodded and lifted the tray, following me from the room. As soon as he set it on the counter, I turned.

"What are you trying to do?" I asked, echoing Jennifer's question from the night before.

"To help," he answered, reaching into the box and pulling out a donut. "All the stuff that happened that summer never sat right with me. I followed the story for a while after, reading newspapers, catching glimpses on the news, hoping to hear anything about Marcus or the others." He poked the donut with his finger then shrugged and took a bite. Raspberry jelly oozed out the side, reminding me of the cave and the red pulsing liquid that'd covered the stump. "Nothing was ever found, and after a while, no one even talked about it anymore."

I shivered.

"Nate? Are you okay?"

"Yeah. I just... look, the whole reason I wanted to go back was to show Jennifer that there's nothing there to be afraid of. You brought all this stuff in and started talking about Sarah, and—"

Brandon held up his hand and a glob of jelly splashed onto the floor. "Whoa. Whoa. That girl lost her sister. She isn't going to forget that just because we walk on eggshells around her. You want to help fix her problems? Justify them; don't ignore them."

"How is it better to have her believe that some boogeyman in the woods took her sister when we both know she was kidnapped by some kind of serial killer or pedophile?"

"Guys."

We both turned. Jennifer stood in the doorway.

"Shit, Jennifer, I'm sorry. I didn't mean—"

She cut me off with a sharp look. "How about you stop trying to decide what I should or shouldn't believe? For Christ's sake, you're worse than my parents and my fucking therapist."

I followed her as she stormed through the apartment into my bedroom. "Come back, okay? I'm sorry."

She unbuttoned my shirt and tossed it on the floor. I glanced away, blushing, trying not to stare at her body. She grabbed her own shirt and pulled it down over her head. "I should've known you weren't actually trying to help me. You don't believe me, just like everyone else. But you know what's worse? You were there, Nate. You were there, and you still don't fucking believe me."

When I finally gathered enough nerve to look at her face, she was crying. I crossed the room in three strides and wrapped my arms around her, pulling her against my chest. "I'm sorry, Jennifer. It's just... a lot. I know you believe this weird monster thing was in the woods—"

"Forest Man," she interrupted.

"Right, Forest Man." The name burned like salt on my tongue. "Stick with me and Brandon, okay? We'll go there and we'll figure out who or whatever did this, and this time we *will* destroy it. I promise."

CHAPTER 15

We didn't stop running until we'd made it back to the lake. By then, the rain had reduced to a fine mist. I bent over, hugging the stitch in my side. I'd never run faster in my life.

"What," Brandon wheezed, "was that?"

"You know what it was." I heaved, but nothing came up.

We stood, catching our breath. My shirt clung to me like a second skin.

After a long, awkward pause, Brandon finally spoke. "Was it Marcus?"

"Yeah," I answered. "It was." My throat ached.

"He's dead."

I wasn't sure what I'd thought. Maybe a small part of me had held out hope that he *was* playing a trick on us, or that he'd just gotten lost in the woods and he'd wander back to the cabins eventually, or maybe the police would find him. I tried to respond, but my voice emerged as a pathetic croak. No matter, Brandon's words hadn't been a question anyway.

They were a statement of fact. Marcus was dead, and his corpse had been there in the cave, singing to us.

"What are we going to do, Nate?"

He was pacing back and forth, tracking footprints across the wet sand.

"We've got to go find Officer Hollis and tell him we found Marcus's body." My knuckles were white from clutching the hatchet.

The storm had passed quickly and now the sun pressed down, drying out my shirt. Despite the growing heat, I couldn't control my shivering.

Brandon followed as I led the way back to the Mathesons' cabin. The police cruiser was parked out front, which meant Hollis was likely still inside with the family.

The cabin's front porch wrapped most of the way around the house, complete with deck chairs and a large gas grill. We stood at the bottom of the stairs, so that the Mathesons wouldn't be able to see us from inside.

I grabbed the banister to help support my shaking legs. There was a rough gash in the wood. I grimaced and pulled my hand back, sure I'd caught a splinter. Carved into the wooden rail was the same shape I'd seen on the boulders outside of the cave.

"Brandon!"

"What is the heck is that?" He tilted his head to get a better view of the carving.

"I don't know, but Jennifer and I saw something like it in the forest. Just outside the cave." I didn't have to explain what cave I meant.

We broke off the conversation when Officer Hollis stepped onto the Mathesons' porch, looking less than pleased to see us. He tipped his hat. "What can I do for you boys?" he asked, eyeing the hatchet in my hand.

"We went back down to the cave," I said. "It was there this time. Marcus was there, too."

The policeman sighed and rubbed his jaw. "Boys, we walked all over those woods. There is no cave."

"There is!" Brandon insisted. "Nate saw it too. It was different, but it was the same cave. We were going to chop down the statue and bring it to show you."

Officer Hollis raised a brow. "Okay, so where is it?"

"We couldn't get it," I explained. "When we tried to destroy it, Marcus came and we ran away."

Officer Hollis exhaled a deep sigh. "I'm taking you back to your parents. We're going to have a talk with them about what you've told me."

I felt a flutter of hope in my chest. Finally, the grownups were going to listen.

CHAPTER 16

When Jennifer finished crying, I did the only thing I could think of; I told her we needed a plan. That meant we needed Brandon and his collection of research.

Brandon had waited patiently on the couch in our absence, and when Jennifer and I emerged from the bedroom, he picked up as though there had been no interruption at all. He had a map spread over the table, with points of interest indicated in red marker.

"According to the layout of the forest around Lake Swart, and based on what I can remember about the geography of the place, the cave should be about here." He pointed to an area east of the lake.

"You'd know better than anyone. You were always drawing up maps of the place."

"Right, but there's one thing that's been bothering me."

"And that is?"

"That we won't be able to find it again," Jennifer answered for him.

I stared down at the little red circle on the map. "Let's consider what we know for sure." I held up a finger. "One, we found a strange cave in the woods our last summer at Lake Swart. "Two," I held up a second finger, "Marcus and Sarah went missing that same summer, and Franklin the summer before."

"Three," Brandon cut in, "there is a history of disappearances all linked to the area."

I rolled my eyes. "Okay, fine. What else do we know?"

"It's all connected to the Forest Man," Jennifer added.

I sighed inwardly. She was already pissed at me for not believing her, but I still couldn't bring myself to consider the possibility that this thing was real. Stumps didn't just come alive and start snatching children. Corpses didn't hide out in caves in the middle of the forest. And even if any of this *was* possible, it didn't explain why the cave had vanished when Brandon led the police there.

"We should also consider what we don't know." Brandon shifted uncomfortably in his seat. "How it works and how to destroy it. We tried chopping it down, but the blade bounced off it like the thing was made of stone."

Jennifer stood, arms folded and lips pressed tight. "We don't know what it does to the people it takes. Do you think by destroying it we'll get them back?"

I knew she was thinking about Sarah. I took her hand and squeezed gently. Whatever had happened that summer, Jennifer blamed herself for Sarah's disappearance. Maybe going back and at least *trying* to do something would be enough to assuage her guilt.

"Any ideas on how to destroy it?" I asked Brandon. "I don't suppose you have a stash of dynamite handy?"

He returned to his stack of papers, sorting until he found the one he wanted. I lifted it from his hands, and tensed when I saw the picture printed on the top. It had been twenty years since I'd seen it, but the image of clasped hands had engraved itself in my memory. I instinctively knew this was the same symbol I'd seen outside the cave and carved into the banister at the Mathesons' cabin. This time the symbol was clearer. There were two hands. One of them was human; the other was something else.

"Well, shit." Cold sweat beaded across my forehead.

"I thought you didn't remember," Jennifer said. I couldn't tell if she was genuinely curious, or being facetious.

"I thought I didn't remember, too." The paper trembled in my hands.

"This symbol is old. I tried finding something similar, or to match it to any existing lore, but there's only so much you can do in one night. I think it has to do with the thing in the cave. The Forest Man." He said the name with lips wrinkled in disgust like it left a bad taste in his mouth.

I hesitated, trying to form a reply. I promised Jennifer I'd destroy this thing. There was no harm in trying. If it wasn't real, then it wouldn't matter if the attempt worked or not. All that mattered was if Jennifer thought it did. "I know someone At Union Grove who might be able to help us."

CHAPTER 17

om stood in the doorway to my room, head in hands. She wouldn't even look at me after Officer Hollis recounted what Brandon and I had said. "Oh, Nate, how could you?" She was on the verge of tears.

I sat on the edge of my waterbed and stared down at my high-top Reeboks. They were covered in mud and detritus from the forest floor. Later, when Mom was less upset about me and Brandon, I knew I was going to get an earful about ruining my shoes. "But Mom, everything we said is true!"

My father paced back and forth across the carpet, with spasms of rage periodically flashing across his face. "Enough." Dad's hushed word filled the room.

My stomach was in my throat. They had demanded an explanation, but couldn't accept the one I'd offered them.

Dad's chest swelled as he inhaled a deep breath. He was a therapist by trade, but my mother insisted he leave it at the door when he came home. Most of the time, he did, but today, in my mind, I could see him transforming from father to therapist, from Dad to doctor. "You were all told to stay out of the police's way, were you not?"

I hated when he asked questions we both knew the answer to. It felt like a sneaky way of squeezing a confession from me. I nodded all the same.

"But you still decided to go into the forest again with Brandon?" His voice rose at the end, forming the accusation into a question.

"We were trying to help!"

"You know better!" He yelled, then rubbed his temples.

I closed my eyes. *You know better* was the ultimate guilt trip, passed down from generation to generation of parents. It wasn't just that I'd done something wrong, but I'd knowingly done something wrong. A distinction that always affected the severity of my punishment.

"I'm sorry, Dad. We thought we were doing the right thing! We were terrified. There's something out there, and no one will listen to us--"

He sighed, exhaling his disappointment. The anger melted from his features. "I believe you."

That was good news, at least.

"Nate." He sat beside me, and the water-filled mattress sunk beneath his weight shifting me over. "I'm worried about you."

Nope, it was bad news.

"I know you kids like to goof around and play, and tell scary stories. I'm not sure what all you've been getting up to, but something has put this idea into your head."

"But, Dad I—"

He held up a hand, and I knew to shut up and let him finish.

"You don't believe in Santa Claus anymore, do you?"

"No," I answered, unable to mask my sulking.

"How about the tooth fairy?"

"No."

"Unicorns?"

I didn't dignify that one with an answer, I just stared forward, willing this talk to be over.

"Right, you know those things are made up. I don't know why, but it's easier for people to believe in bad things than good."

"Wait, what?"

He smiled with sadness in his eyes. "We stop believing in the good things, but we hold on to the bad things. Mothman, Bigfoot, Chupacabra, the Jersey Devil? They're all monsters that some people believe exist. But if you asked those same people if they believed in mermaids or dragons, they'd probably tell you they didn't."

I waited for my thoughts to catch up with what I was hearing. I studied his face. He was older than I remembered, which struck me as funny, since I saw him almost every day. His hair was thin at the top and gray on the sides. Wisdom reflected in his pale eyes. "Why?"

He patted my shoulder. "Well, son. I think it's because some of us outgrow magic and wonder, but we never outgrow fear. Not entirely."

It was the first time he'd spoken to me like an adult. My chest swelled with pride. He was right. There was no such thing as the Easter Bunny or the Loch Ness Monster, and there was no such thing as the Forest Man, either.

"I'm sure you saw something," he continued. "I know you, and you wouldn't make up a story like this. But, Nate, whatever you think you saw wasn't real. You and your friends were frightened, and you worked each other into a frenzy. I'm not at all surprised you think you saw a monster in the woods."

He stood up to go and his hand clasped my shoulder. "Do Mom a favor and clean the mud off those shoes before you track a mess through the house. Okay, pal?"

I nodded and slipped off my sneakers without bothering to untie them.

CHAPTER 18

I parked my Subaru in the faculty lot at Union Groove. Brandon followed in his Rubicon, occupying the spot beside me.

"They won't really tow me for parking here, will they?" he asked, glancing at the *Faculty Parking Only All Others Will be Towed* sign.

"Nah. It's pretty quiet on campus in the summer. You should be fine."

Jennifer climbed out of the passenger's side and examined the campus buildings. "So, where do we find this doctor whoever, anyway?"

She sounded like one of my students.

"Dr. *Coleridge's* office is in the atrium."

Jennifer nodded and turned towards the building to our left.

It wasn't a large campus, but she didn't hesitate before choosing the right direction. "How do you know where the atrium is?"

She favored me with one of her rare *real* smiles. "I took classes here a few years back, Professor."

My knees threatened to give out from under me. "You didn't take my class, did you? No, I would have recognized you. Your name at least."

She actually laughed. It was beautiful and musical. Every cliché I'd ever heard or read about love burst to life in that moment. Love, not just a childhood crush.

I didn't have time to consider the repercussions of my epiphany before we were climbing the stairs to Dr. Coleridge's office. The door was a collage of bulletins advertising student organization meetings and old Far Side comics. Her office door was open just a crack. I tapped gently and stuck my face in the gap. "Anyone home?"

She glanced up from the stack of papers on her desk, peering out over the top of her glasses. "Nice to see you, Nate." She nodded politely at Jennifer and Brandon as they crept in behind me. Her office was a mess of folders and papers littered over every surface. There was a small blue sofa in the corner, long buried beneath stacks of books and research notes. "To what do I owe the pleasure?"

"These are old friends of mine," I explained. "Jennifer and Brandon."

She nodded, sending gray curls cascading down over her forehead. "It's nice to meet you both."

"I'm sorry to bother you, Susan, but we were doing some research into the area, and I was hoping you might be able to help us." I glanced back at Brandon, who was pulling a sheet free from the manilla folder tucked under his arm.

She settled her wireframe glasses back onto her nose and accepted the paper from Brandon. "This is local?"

"Yeah," Jennifer answered. "We saw this symbol in a forest near here when we were kids."

Susan lifted a brow. "So, this is more than idle curiosity, then?"

I grimaced. I'd made it a habit to never discuss personal matters with my colleagues. I'd have to choose my words carefully. "Sort of. We started... reminiscing about when we were kids, and it came up. We all saw this symbol there, in the woods, and wondered if it meant something." I glanced up at her, but she was engrossed by the images on the paper.

"What woods?" she asked.

"Around Lake Swart," I answered.

"I'm familiar with the area," she began, then glanced at Brandon and Jennifer. "My specialty is precolonial America in the northeast region." She pointed to the overstuffed bookshelf against the wall. "Third shelf, second book from the right with the red spine, please." Brandon scanned the shelves, grabbed the volume, and handed it to her. She opened it and started flipping pages, her eyes not moving from the images on Brandon's paper.

"Local legends record the area surrounding the lake as a significant religious site," Dr. Coleridge said.

"What does that mean?" Jennifer asked.

"Like a temple or a church. A place where spiritual practices and rituals are observed." She pushed the book towards us and pointed to a page. "When white settlers moved into the area, some of them began to worship those older gods, too."

"Older gods?" I asked. I had a degree in history, for fuck's sake. If any of this was real, I should have known about it.

"Sorry, Miss..." Brandon began.

"Doctor," she corrected. "Or you can call me Susan."

"Sorry, Doctor, there was something else. In the forest, with the markings. There was an odd statue, sculpture, thing."

I glared a warning at him. It was one thing to discuss Forest Man amongst ourselves, but I didn't need my coworkers knowing about the crazy.

"What did the statue look like?" she asked. Her attention had turned back to the open book.

"Like a tree stump with a face," Jennifer answered.

"And arms," Brandon added.

I rubbed my temples. I should have insisted on taking care of this myself.

"We think," I said, stepping in. "We were young when we saw these things. We may not be remembering details correctly."

"I'm not surprised," Dr. Coleridge explained, "it isn't odd for totems or statues to be used in conjunction with rites and rituals. We still use them today in modern religious practice. Think about your statues of Christ on the cross, or crucifixes."

Academic curiosity, at least, was better than incredulity.

"The symbol here is a sigil," Susan said, gesturing to Brandon's paper.

"What are sigils?" Brandon asked.

"Symbols associated with magic or sometimes spiritual practices. Believed by some to have power between the spiritual and physical realms. What they are purported to do, and how they work, varies by who placed them."

"Do you think they're connected to the Forest Man?" Jennifer asked.

"Forest Man?" Dr. Coleridge echoed.

"Sorry, Susan," I jumped in before either of them could make it sound worse. "That's the nickname we gave the sculpture... or stump... when we were children."

"Ah. Well, it must be. It would be a rather bizarre coincidence otherwise, don't you think?"

"Right." I stuck out my hand, and Susan shook it. "Thanks for your help."

"I'll try to find more answers for you. Come back and see me soon."

Jennifer and Brandon followed me back down the atrium stairs.

"So now what?" Jennifer asked.

Dark thoughts of what was waiting for us at Lake Swart crept into my mind. Whether or not *it* was real, the memories were real enough, and those alone might be our undoing. "Now we go back, and see if we can find it."

"But we don't know how to destroy it yet." Her voice trembled.

"How to destroy it won't matter if we can't find it. Let's go back and get a good look at it. We'll study the symbol, too, and by the time we've found it again, maybe Susan will have discovered something that can help us."

We climbed in our cars and left Union Grove behind, heading back to Lake Swart for the first time in twenty years. "You have the keys to your parents' cabin?" I asked Jennifer.

She held them up and nodded.

CHAPTER 19

My parents were already packing.

"We can't leave. Not while Marcus is missing." I'd tried begging and pleading, but I knew nothing was going to convince them. Especially not after what Brandon and I had done.

My mom frowned, tucking a folded blouse into her Samsonite case. "We can't help by staying, and what if there's a kidnapper or someone out there? It's dangerous. The police have cleared us, so we're leaving tomorrow."

"Mom, I—"

"Don't argue with your mother, young man. We're leaving, and that's our final decision. I'm sorry that you can't stay and play with your friends, but the other families are leaving too. There's no point in being here any longer."

Stay and play with your friends?

Did they think this was all just some kind of game to them?

His father's words were like a slap in the face. Franklin's disappearance hadn't felt real, probably because none of us had been there when it happened. None of us but Marcus, anyway. It was easy to pretend it hadn't happened. But the grownups must have known, hadn't they?

"Did you guys know about Franklin?"

My parents exchanged a knowing glance, demonstrating the near-telepathic connection only married couples seemed to have.

"Nate…" my father began, abandoning his rolled-up boxer shorts on the bed.

"I want to know," I insisted. "You just said it's too dangerous to stay here, but you knew about Franklin and you came back anyway. If you really thought it was dangerous, you wouldn't have come."

"We knew about Franklin," he answered. "The police called us after he went missing to ask a few questions."

"What kind of questions?"

He sat on the edge of the bed. "Mostly they wanted to know about the other families that were here and if we'd seen anyone suspicious. We thought whatever happened to Franklin was an accident, that maybe he'd gotten lost in the forest or there was an accident on the lake." He grimaced when he said the last.

"And now?" I asked, already knowing, yet dreading the answer.

He placed a hand on my shoulder. "We already talked about monsters, right?"

I swallowed hard and nodded.

"Well, I wasn't entirely honest about monsters, Nate. Some of them do exist, but they are always the human kind.

If it had just been one child that vanished, it could be written off as an accident, but now… it seems clear that someone has done this. We need to leave and get you kids out of harm's way until they can catch whoever's doing this."

"What about Jennifer's family?" I asked.

He nodded. "Leaving tomorrow."

"Can I at least say goodbye?"

"Sure, son," he said, laying a hand on my shoulder that was cold comfort. "Tomorrow."

CHAPTER 20

The asphalt ended abruptly at the private drive leading to Lake Swart. A Toyota Prius with fogged windows sat parked in front of the padlocked iron gate marking the entrance to the long-abandoned community. There were no signs of life beyond the gate. Not that I'd expected it; Brandon had told us the community closed after too many disappearances. Most had been explained away as accidents, but bad luck had a way of festering and causing people to avoid certain places through intuition.

"You coming?" I asked Jennifer, reaching for the door handle.

She'd grown silent as we approached the lake. Almost in a trance, the way I remembered from that summer. "Not yet."

"Are you sure you're up for this?"

She nodded.

"Okay. I'm gonna go get that gate open. Sit tight."

I followed as Brandon approached the parked car and tapped on the window. After a moment, the window lowered and a teenage boy's face appeared. Just past him, in the passenger's seat, was a blonde pimple-faced boy of similar age.

"What are you kids doing out here?" Brandon asked with the authority of a stern parent.

"Uh, we were just talking, Sir."

"Do a lot of kids come out here to... talk?" Brandon asked.

"No," he answered. "Most people are afraid to come out here. They say the lake is haunted, or something." From his tone, he clearly didn't believe it.

Brandon nodded down the road. "Why don't you kids get going?"

"Who are you?" the pimply boy in the passenger's seat asked.

"The ghost of summers past," I replied.

Brandon smirked as the car started and turned off towards the main road, leaving us there alone to stare at our past, just behind the gate.

"I don't suppose you know how to pick locks?" I asked.

He held up a finger and disappeared around the back of his Jeep. After a moment, he emerged, hefting a pair of bolt cutters.

"What the hell, man? Trespass much?" Jennifer still had the keys to her parents' cabin, but that didn't make popping the lock feel less criminal.

Brandon grinned. He looked just as he had when we were twelve. "Be prepared, Nate."

Something in his tone made me feel like everything might be all right. I was almost glad we'd returned.

Almost.

The wail of a struggling engine screeched from down the street. I closed my eyes. I'd forgotten about Lee.

A white Ford F250 held together by rust and prayers pulled off the side of the road. If the truck was younger than me, it wasn't by much. The bumper sported a bright yellow *Don't Tread on Me* sticker, the only thing about the truck that looked even remotely new.

Lee climbed from the cab. I wouldn't have recognized him if I hadn't been expecting him. His chin was sharp as a razor, and his cheekbones hollow and gaunt. He looked twenty years older than he should have. His hair had gone prematurely gray. It was funny to think this was the person we'd been afraid of as kids, the one who'd bullied us into submission.

"Nate." He nodded. "It's been a long time."

"Yeah. Yeah, it has."

"Is Jenny with you?" he asked.

I pursed my lips and cast a furtive glance at my car.

He followed my gaze, then turned his attention to the bolt cutters in Brandon's hands. "Shit yeah, breaking and entering. And here I thought this trip was gonna be lame as fuck."

"It isn't technically breaking in," I said, feeling twelve years old all over again. "Jennifer's family still owns the cabin. It's private property."

Lee spat a brown stream of tobacco. "Tell that to them." He hitched a finger towards the *No Trespassing* sign tacked on a large oak on the other side of the gate.

"We've got more important things to worry about than that," Brandon answered.

Lee smirked and turned to me. "So, uh, you and Jenny bumping uglies or what?"

My ears burned crimson. "Why do you care?" Jesus, I *was* twelve again.

"I didn't want to cut in if you were... you know. But if you're not, she and I used to have thing, and I was thinking, well..." He winked, and every muscle in my hand twitched.

Before I could answer, there was a snapping sound followed by the clank of a chain slithering to the ground.

"We're in," Brandon said.

CHAPTER 21

I ran straight to Jennifer's cabin the next morning, relieved when I saw her parents' car still in the drive. I knocked at the door, then sat on the steps, waiting, but no one answered.

I figured they must be sleeping in and decided to tap on Jennifer's window. I couldn't leave without saying goodbye. Without telling her how I felt. I'd ask for her phone number. Maybe we could arrange to see each other over the summer.

She slid the window open after a few taps. The timid way she glanced at me and the ashen pallor of her face tugged at my heart.

"Are you leaving today, too?" I asked.

She shrugged. "We were going to, but we probably won't. My parents will want to stay and look for Sarah."

"What do you mean 'look for Sarah'?" I saw a shadow in the room behind her. I stood on my tiptoes and caught a flash of red bandana. Lee. Lee was in Jennifer's room.

"She's gone. She went to play with the Forest Man. She

won't come back; they never do. But don't be sad, she won't be alone. She'll be with Franklin and Marcus."

"Jennifer, did you tell your parents? Why is Lee here?"

She nodded. "I told them all about the Forest Man. They don't believe me; they think I'm crazy, but I told them... I gave Him Sarah's book. He needed it so He could find her and bring her to stay with Him." She tugged at her hair. Her face held no expression, but her eyes...her eyes shone with that same fear I'd seen the day before.

"Why is Lee here?" I repeated.

"He believes me about the Forest Man. Lee saw him too, he's the only one that understands."

Lee stepped forward and wrapped an arm around her shoulders, pulling her away from the window. "Come on, Jenny." He flashed a menacing smile. "Nate's leaving."

"No, Jennifer, wait!"

Lee lowered the window and pulled the drapes, shutting me out of her life for good.

CHAPTER 22

Do you want to unpack first, or head straight down to the cave?" Brandon asked. It was early evening; we only had a few hours of daylight left.

I looked over my shoulder. Jennifer stood by the car, speaking when spoken to and moving when prompted. I felt a pang of guilt. Maybe I'd pushed her too hard. "We should probably unpack. I think she needs some time. Meanwhile, Lee can fill us in on what he remembers from that summer."

Lee's eyes went dark and he didn't reply.

"Surely you remember something?" Brandon asked.

He spit a brown stream into the dust. "Is this the part where I tell you not to call me Shirley?"

I sighed, grabbing the bags from my trunk.

Jennifer had wandered up the stairs, already turning the key in the lock.

Lee grabbed my shoulder, tight. "What did you do to her? Is she okay?"

I jerked out of his grasp. "I didn't do shit. The closer

we got to the lake, the more spaced out she got. Like that summer."

Lee turned, and I noticed a rolled-up notebook protruding from his back pocket.

"Hey…" I grabbed it and tugged. "This reminds me. That summer, you took a notebook from Marcus's room."

He jerked it from my grip and looked around nervously. "Not out here. Let's go inside."

Brandon and I followed him up the stairs. I noticed Lee hadn't brought any bags.

We tracked footprints across the dusty hardwood floor. Light filtered in through the cabin's windows, catching on the cobwebs that hung from the ceiling like streamers. No one had been here in years, that much was certain. I flipped a switch on the wall, but no light came on.

"Hey Jenny, do your parents still pay the electric for this place?" Lee asked.

She stood silent by the large kitchen window, looking out in the direction of the forest.

"We oughta search for candles and such," I said. "Did anyone bring flashlights?"

Brandon unzipped his duffle and pulled out a pair of Maglite flashlights along with a few smaller LEDs and a battery powered camping lantern.

I grinned and shook my head. "Let me guess. Be prepared?"

He nodded once.

We eventually produced enough matches and candles to supplement Brandon's lantern and keep the place lit after dark.

"Did you bring food?"

"I'm glad you asked." Brandon ducked out of the kitchen and returned with a small camping stove.

After everything was arranged, I sat down at the table, nodding to the chairs across from me. Lee and Brandon sat. "We're set for tonight."

Jennifer stood vigil by the window, staring out as if waiting for something. I wondered what she was searching for.

"We'll head into the woods in the morning. Is that the notebook?" I asked Lee, nodding at the wadded-up mess in his hand.

He grimaced and tossed it onto the table. "Yeah, it is."

"What's in it?"

He tilted his chin towards it. "See for yourself."

The first page of the notebook, now creased and yellowed, had a rough sketch of the tree stump. It looked much as I'd remembered, the bark shaped like a face. No wonder we'd been terrified; it was creepy. Underneath the sketch were the words *Forest Man*, written like a label. A name.

I flipped the page. The words to that song we'd heard in the cave were scrawled there in red ink. At least, I hoped it was ink. I could feel the color draining from my face. I felt a paralyzing fear, like I was twelve all over again. Why had I come back here? What the hell was I trying to prove?

I flipped another page. There was a sketch of a boy done in pencil. It was little more than a stick figure with a UFO drawn on the t-shirt. The stick figure was touching... holding...a piece of the tree stump. I slammed the book shut.

"What the hell is this, Lee?" Brandon asked, sliding the book towards him and flipping through the pages.

"It is what it is." He flashed his usual non-committal smirk.

I felt everything go red. I wasn't a little boy anymore. My hands shook as I reached across the table to grab his collar. "You listen to me, you fucking asshole. I've had it with your bullshit! You tell me what happened, or I'll beat it out of you."

His eyes widened. I saw my face reflected in them, and I looked furious. He pulled himself free of my grip. "Okay, okay. Calm down."

"Talk. Now."

He gave a sigh, heavy with years of baggage. "Forest Man is its name."

I rolled my eyes. "Not this bullshit again."

"Shut up and listen."

Brandon put a hand on my shoulder. "Hear him out, Nate."

"Something happened to me and Jenny out there. I don't know why it was us and not you or Brandon. But...the thing, it came after us."

"A person? Someone hiding in the woods?"

"No, not like that. We both started having dreams after we were in the cave. Me after the first time, and her after she went with you. He'd come to us in those dreams, holding out His hand, singing that damned song. 'Come play!' He said. Sometimes He was alone. Sometimes, He came with Franklin, but it was wrong. Franklin was all covered in blood. He looked torn...Eaten. I don't know."

I jumped when Jennifer pulled out a chair to sit down.

I'd been so engrossed in Lee's story that I hadn't noticed her leave the window.

She sighed and looked up at me. "It was the same with me, but Marcus was there too. Franklin was all rotted and gross, like a zombie movie or something. When he tried to talk, maggots fell out of his mouth. I heard words in my head. 'Come play...' He asked if I wanted to play. I said...I said no. But then He told me that if I wouldn't play with Him, He'd be lonely, and He'd take us all. So, He told me to pick. To pick someone to come and play."

She lay her head on the table and sobbed. Lee put his arm around her, murmuring softly.

"You picked Sarah, didn't you?" Brandon asked.

"We had a fight, and I was upset. I didn't know—"

I turned to Lee. "And you? You picked Marcus."

He nodded, not meeting my eyes.

"No, no. This isn't..." I struggled for the right words. "You guys didn't do this. Maybe you had nightmares, or maybe you don't remember right, but there is no way that either of you did this."

Brandon cradled his head in his hands. "So, you think it's all a coincidence? That they had these dreams... these visions? And then what they dreamed came true?"

"No. But people forget things, and people invent memories." I glanced at Jennifer. "How long have you been on meds?"

She wiped her nose on her arm. "Since I was a teenager."

"See? We can't trust these memories." I had to believe they weren't true, otherwise it had been Marcus who'd chased us out of the cave all those years ago. I wasn't ready for that to be real.

CHAPTER 23

Brandon thumbed through the notebook, taking in the details of each page. I watched Jennifer, who alternated between pacing the length of the kitchen and staring out the window.

Lee had taken up residence on the mildewy sofa in the living room.

Brandon tilted the book towards me. "These are the same ones, aren't they?" he asked, indicating a drawing of the symbol we'd seen on the boulders in the forest.

"Yeah. Pretty close, if not exact."

Jennifer stopped pacing. Her eyes locked on the page. "That was Marcus's?"

Brandon nodded and turned the book towards her.

"You said you saw Marcus in that cave after he died, right?" she asked, staring at the page.

Brandon cleared his throat. "I did, yes. Nate said he didn't remember."

I grimaced.

"I saw him too." She glanced up at Brandon. I felt a pang of jealousy.

"In the cave?" he asked.

She shook her head. "No. Here. After I... oh, God." She bent over, sobbing.

I jumped from my chair and wrapped my arms around her. "Shhh. It's okay." I ran a hand through her oily hair.

She sniffled and turned her head away from me. "After I left Sarah's book for Him. That night I was looking out the window and I saw Marcus. He came out of the woods and stood there, staring at the cabin."

Suddenly I understood why she'd spent so much time staring out the window since we arrived. She was waiting for Marcus, or maybe even Sarah, to appear.

"Did he say anything to you?" Brandon asked.

"No. He just stared, and then I got scared, so I ran to my room and hid in my closet."

Brandon drummed his fingers on the tabletop. "It doesn't make sense. Why would he appear to you *after* you gave them Sarah's book?"

"Because he wasn't there for her," I answered, walking over to the window. A white-tailed chipmunk skittered across the overgrown lawn. "Sarah's bedroom is on this side of the house, Jennifer's is on the opposite side. He was here for Sarah."

I hadn't meant to say it out loud. It wasn't like I actually believed any of this nonsense. A thick blanket of silence settled over the room as the implications of my statement sank in.

"I think I need to lie down," Jennifer said, shaking a pill from her bottle and popping it into her mouth. She grabbed one of the sleeping bags from the pile on the floor and vanished down the hall.

"Think she's going to her bedroom?" Lee asked, sitting up on the couch.

I scowled. "Leave her alone."

"Did it ever occur to you that she might want company?"

"No," I answered. "She needs time to think shit through for herself. You aren't going to go in there and take advantage of her like you did last time."

He at least had the good grace to look surprised by the accusation. "Last time?"

"Yeah, that last summer we were here. I came to check on her. To say goodbye, and you were there in her room."

The corner of his lip curled. "She was scared. She needed someone, and I didn't see either of you sacking up to go take care of her."

"Why do you think I was there?"

Lee shrugged. "I don't know and I don't care."

"I don't understand the two of you anyway." My body trembled. "I mean, you never seemed to notice her before that. Why the sudden interest? What happened?" I didn't want the answers, but I needed them. I needed to understand why.

Lee pried himself from the sofa's grasp and crossed the kitchen, standing at the edge of the table. "None of you knew it that summer, but Sarah and me? We had a thing. When you weren't around, we were fooling around. She even let me get to second base, man."

I wanted to tell him to stop, that I didn't want to hear anymore, but my mouth wouldn't obey my brain's command.

"So, when she went missing, I figured what the hell, her sister would do. I mean it's pretty much the same thing, right?"

I wasn't a wimpy little kid anymore. I could finally do what I'd been waiting years to do. I launched myself out of the chair towards Lee, determined to make him pay for every bit of pain and heartache he'd caused me. Brandon grabbed me by the shoulder and jerked me back before my fist made contact.

Lee laughed. "You always were easy to get riled up."

"Stop it," Brandon said to Lee, "or I'll let him go. I'll wager he could take you now."

Lee rolled his eyes and went back to the sofa.

I grabbed my sleeping bag and unrolled it in the hallway outside Jennifer's bedroom door. The only way Lee was getting in there was over my dead body.

CHAPTER 24

Within the dusty confines of the cabin's hallway, I lay staring at the ceiling. I tried counting sheep and counting backwards from one hundred, but my body refused to relax, so I seethed instead.

Fucking Lee. It was always fucking Lee. He'd meant to scare me that day at Jennifer's window, and he'd succeeded, but he wasn't scary anymore. He was just some dried-up white trash redneck who got off making other people feel like shit.

I stewed in anger and discomfort, tossing and turning. I should've taken one of the other bedrooms, like Brandon had, or at least a soft piece of furniture, like Lee, but I needed to protect Jennifer. Thoughts I wouldn't have entertained days ago formed in the back of my mind and crept their way into my consciousness.

I rolled over on my side, facing Jennifer's bedroom door. She certainly believed, and she'd clung to Lee because he also believed. Hell, even Brandon believed. This was some sort of shared delusion between the three of them. Lee had been in Jennifer's room that last day at the lake when she was out of it. He could have done something to her. But that didn't account for Brandon. I was the odd man out here. The outsider. And yet, half-remembered visions of the oozing stump and Marcus's ruined eye haunted me.

It was crazy to think the thing in the forest cave could be real. It was crazy to think that all of this had come from one simple delusion. It was crazy, period.

Unless it wasn't. And the implications of that were nothing less than terrifying.

Enough was enough. There was only one way to find out.

I moved quickly, pushing my sleeping bag off and creeping into the kitchen. I grabbed one of Brandon's Maglites and pushed the side door open.

The night air was damp and cool, like the air after a storm, though it hadn't rained in days. The moon wasn't quite full, but reflected enough light to navigate the darkness. I saw the large erratics that marked the start of the Boulder Path, and I entered the forest.

Tall weeds had taken over portions of the trail. No one had been this way in years. I jumped each time a twig snapped beneath my feet. I should've waited for morning and come with the others, but I needed to get out of the stifling dusty air of the cabin. I needed to get away from Lee. Everything about him kept me on edge and made my blood simmer.

I arrived at a spot on the trail that didn't look familiar, but felt *right*. I knew it was the place. I veered off in what I hoped was the direction of the cave.

The blood drained from my face as that ominous maw gaped open, welcoming me inside to be devoured. I swept the flashlight's beam over the lichen-covered boulders outside the cave. The weathering of the stones had created grooves and hollows. Last time, the marks had been obvious, and though I was no geologist, even I knew twenty years wasn't long enough for this much erosion. I ran a hand over the stone, flecking off pieces of lichen like dried skin. My fingers brushed a crevice in the stone, arched into a semi-circle. I brushed off the lichen and lit the boulder's surface with the flashlight.

It was as I recalled. The same, almost exactly, as the image we'd given Dr. Coleridge. The symbol had something to do with the Forest Man. A sigil, she'd called it. A link between the spiritual and material worlds. Did that make the stump some sort of spirit entity? I wasn't sure. I inhaled a deep breath, and stepped towards the cave.

As I inched closer, the inside of the cave came into focus. The tree stump loomed just past the entrance; except this time, it was surrounded by trinkets. Necklaces, bracelets, keychains, keys, car fobs, cell phones, even a hoodie—all draped around it like offerings at an altar.

A twig snapped behind me, and I froze.

"Nate?" Lee's voice tremored.

"Yeah."

"I'll be damned," he said, staring into the cave. "I half imagined it wouldn't be here. That it never was here."

"Are you alone?" I asked.

"Yeah, I heard you sneaking out. I thought you might

be going out for a smoke. When I realized where you were going, I thought I'd follow."

"Sarah's book." I said, staring down at a rectangle covered in black mold and propped against the stump. It had all been real.

"What?" Lee asked.

"Sarah was reading a book that summer. Nancy Drew, I think. When I found Jennifer here, she'd left the book. That's how she chose Sarah. She left the book." I turned to face him. Anger wrapped its fist tightly around my chest, causing my heart to race. "Which means you took something from Marcus, didn't you?"

He rubbed the back of his neck.

"Answer me!"

"Yeah, all right? Yes. I nicked a keychain from his pocket that night at the beach. I brought it down here. Look, I didn't think it was real. I thought I was dreaming. I thought he was messing with us, and I was mad, okay? I figured if we came back down here and he saw his keychain it would freak him out."

"But then he went missing," I continued. "He went missing and you knew, but you didn't say anything. You let us all believe he was trying to scare us, but you knew the truth!" I stepped closer, closing the distance between us.

"I didn't know anything for sure, Nate! I was just a kid."

"Just a kid?" I mocked his pleading tone as he recoiled. I advanced on him, delighting in his fear of me—this sudden turn of the tables. He had it coming.

My hands clenched into fists. Lee. Fucking Lee. He was

responsible for what happened to Marcus, and for what happened to Jennifer. And now he thought he could just shrink back and close those drapes on me again?

He brought his hands up around his head, ready for the punch I so desperately wanted to deliver.

Instead, I passed him by, thrusting my shoulder into his. Knocked off-center, he went down to the ground on his knees.

I kept walking deeper into the cave.

"What are you gonna do, man?" For the first time in all the years I'd known him, he looked afraid. Whether it was the thing in the cave that scared him most, or me, I wasn't sure.

I stalked into the cave. He trailed behind me, trying to grab me, to stop me. I shook him off, and when I reached that ancient thing in the cave, I took hold of the tree branch that looked so much like a hand, withdrew something from my pocket, and pressed it into Forest Man's woody claw.

"I'm going to play."

CHAPTER 25

That night, Forest Man came to me in my dreams. Franklin, Marcus, and Sarah were all with Him, but there were others, too. Children I didn't recognize. They sang to me, taunted me, and offered me things. In tattered clothing, they danced circles around me, waving their emaciated limbs in the air.

"Come play!" they sang. "Come play!"

I shook them off. "I can't play with you; I have to take care of Jennifer."

The Forest Man stared down at me, millipedes marching in and out of His eye sockets.

"If you won't come and play with me, who will?"

I fingered a white Bic lighter in my pocket. A lighter that Lee had dropped inside the cave all those years ago, and I already knew the answer.

Jerking upright from the sleeping bag, my back screamed in agony. I hadn't had this kind of nightmare since that summer. I stood and stretched my back, aching and groaning like a man twice my age.

I stumbled over my sleeping bag. My feet felt oddly heavy. A glance at my feet made me realize I still wore my sneakers. I'd been exhausted and must've forgotten to take them off. It was nothing more complex than that.

One of Brandon's Maglites lay tangled in my sleeping bag. I reached down and picked it up, turning it over in my hand. I couldn't remember why I'd had it. A trip outside to relieve myself, maybe?

Brandon was already in the kitchen, boiling water on the camping stove.

"Thank God. I'm useless without caffeine." I said, scooping instant coffee granules from the tin into one of the small metal mugs he'd brought.

"Do you know where Lee got off to?" he asked.

White-hot pain shot through my hand. I'd missed the mug, and poured the scalding water over my hand instead. "Shit! Son of a bitch!" I shook my hand, sending droplets of water flying across the table.

"Something wrong?" Jennifer asked, suppressing a yawn.

"Besides Nate being a klutz?" Brandon shrugged. "Lee's gone."

"Did he get scared and back out?" I asked. My stomach was in knots. The dream lingered in the back of my mind.

"No, his truck's still here," Brandon answered.

"Then he's probably off getting high or something." He had to be. Dreams weren't real.

But thoughts crept in that I couldn't silence. Why

would I sleep in my shoes? Why was the flashlight in my sleeping bag?

Brandon slid a mug across the table for Jennifer. "Have some coffee, then we'll head out for the forest."

"Without Lee?" she asked.

Brandon shrugged. "I'm sure we'll find him wandering around out there somewhere."

CHAPTER 26

We set off down the Boulder Path. It was overgrown, as it had been in my dream, but the forest looked ordinary in the morning's light. Stands of Queen Anne's lace and black-eyed Susans mingled and danced in the sunshine. Nothing marked this place as special or different. We could've been in any forest in New Jersey. Eventually, what little of the path remained was swallowed by underbrush and covered in thick cords of poison ivy.

"This place is probably infested with ticks," Brandon said, brushing off the legs of his khakis.

Jennifer cupped her hands around her mouth. "Lee! Are you out here?"

Anxiety and strong black coffee had me on edge since the moment we'd walked out of the cabin. My mind played out wild scenarios regarding the dream, the shoes, and the flashlight. No wonder we'd been so keyed up that summer. "You know he's probably fucking with us, right?" I snapped.

She lowered her hands with a frown. "He wouldn't do that to me. Not after what we went through here."

"I wouldn't put it past him," I grumbled.

"What the hell is your problem, Nate?"

It felt like a slap. "*My* problem?"

"Yeah," she answered. "Ever since we got here, you've been treating him like shit, starting arguments, threatening him. He went through something that summer, too."

I folded my arms across my chest. "Don't you remember how much he tormented us that summer? He bullied us! He attacked Brandon and he took advantage of you."

She laughed, but it wasn't the musical, wind chime sound. This laugh was harsh and cold. "Is that what you think? You think I can't make my own decisions?"

"Maybe not when you were twelve and crazy with grief!"

"At least he never called me crazy." She spun on her heel and headed back up the path.

"Jennifer, stop. I didn't mean you're crazy, I meant that grief—"

"Guys!" Brandon held up a hand. "The arguing isn't helping. We need to find the cave, and we need to find Lee. Why don't we split up and search? Jennifer, go east. Nate, go west. I'll head north. Don't go too far, stay within shouting distance. We'll meet back here in twenty minutes. Okay?"

Jennifer headed in the direction Brandon had pointed out as east, not bothering to say another word to either of us. As I turned westward, Brandon's hand caught my shoulder.

"What?" I asked, a little too sharply.

"Man, you've got to calm down. Lee isn't the enemy here."

"Says you."

"And her." He nodded in the direction Jennifer had disappeared. "You're making yourself look as bad as him."

I blew out a sigh and nodded. "I'm sorry. Being here again has messed me up. I think maybe I'm remembering things, and then I had this fucked up dream last night."

"Hey man, you don't owe me an apology. But you might owe her one. Twenty minutes, all right?"

"Yeah," I said, heading west into the forest.

Jennifer's voice echoed through the forest. Every few minutes, I could hear her calling out for Lee, and each time, my heart sank a little deeper in my chest. Would she care if it had been me that'd gone missing instead?

The unease I'd felt all morning began to lift. With Lee vanishing, and the lingering memory of my nightmare, I'd almost convinced myself I'd done something unspeakable. But now, in the fresh air and sunshine, I realized that was impossible. We couldn't find the path to the cave because it didn't exist.

CHAPTER 27

The morning's chill faded as the sun rose higher in the sky, sending beads of sweat down the back of my neck. The air was thick with humidity and swarms of gnats and mosquitos took turns assaulting my face when I dared stand still for more than a moment.

We met back at the rendezvous point after twenty minutes, then split up in separate directions again. There was still no sign of Lee, or the cave.

The longer we searched, the lighter I felt. I'd known all along that Forest Man wasn't real, hadn't I? I'd tried to convince Jennifer it didn't exist, and now, as we wandered the forest finding no traces of anything, I couldn't help but hope that some kind of healing process could begin for her.

This was what I'd wanted. The whole reason for coming here had been to show her there was nothing to be afraid of. We'd been frightened children with overactive imaginations.

"I don't understand," she said when we met back on the path after the third search. She'd stopped calling out for Lee after the second.

"I do," Brandon said. "It's like that summer. Remember when I brought the police out here? They couldn't find anything either."

"Yeah, so?" I asked. "Isn't that just proof we were imagining it?"

"What if it works differently for kids?"

I snorted. "What if it's Occam's razor?"

"What's that?" Jennifer asked. It was the first she'd spoken to me since our argument.

"It basically means that the simplest explanation is the most likely."

"And what's that?" she asked.

"The simplest explanation is that Forest Man isn't real. It's something we imagined, hallucinated, or made up. That's why the police couldn't find it then and why we can't find it now. That makes a lot more sense to me than a cave and a stump man that has some kind of magical power to appear and disappear at will."

"Except we didn't imagine Lee vanishing," she retorted, pulling her cigarette pack from her pocket and shaking one loose. It was the first I'd seen her smoke since yesterday.

I bit back my thoughts regarding Lee. After our argument earlier, I didn't want to risk setting her off again. "Either way, we aren't going to find it out here parading around all afternoon. Why don't we go back to the cabin and see if Lee ever showed up there?"

A shiver traveled up my spine at the thought of Lee. There was no cave, which meant it was just a dream, which meant I couldn't have possibly done anything to him. But the light in the sleeping bag and the shoes on my feet when I woke begged to differ.

Brandon nodded. "Good idea. We should regroup and decide what our next move is going to be."

"And clean ourselves up," I added, catching the whiff of an unpleasant odor radiating from my armpits.

Jennifer took one last look around, as if she expected Lee to suddenly pop out of the underbrush. I didn't blame her, it seemed like something he would've done when we were kids.

The path back to the cabin was tread in silence. Even the cicadas seemed to sense our unease and ceased their droning buzz.

As we approached the road back to the lake, Jennifer called for Lee again. "I don't understand. It can't just be a coincidence."

Brandon tried the door to Lee's truck. "It's unlocked. Keys are still in the ignition."

"Guess he wasn't afraid of someone stealing it out here," I said, glancing around.

There was a popping noise, followed by Brandon's low whistle "He's got quite a stash in the glove box."

"He wouldn't have left that behind," Jennifer said, puffing on either her second or third cigarette in a row.

Brandon slid out of the truck's cab. "It's got half a tank of gas. The tires look all right. If he was going to leave, he could've taken it."

"So what if he didn't take the truck? He could've walked." I suggested.

"Walked where?" Jennifer asked. "Where would he have gone in the middle of the night?"

"I've already told you what I think," I answered. "I think he came out here, used a little too much of that stash, and got lost in the woods."

"Then why didn't we find him?" she asked. "If he was lost out there, we would have seen him, or he would've heard us."

"Not if he's sleeping it off somewhere. We didn't even check the other cabins before we left. He could've decided to go rifling through them to see if anyone left behind something valuable."

"Guys," Brandon's voice was flat, emotionless.

Jennifer and I turned.

He was staring at the back of Lee's truck. "I know why we couldn't find him."

CHAPTER 28

Jennifer gasped when she saw the mark. Her cigarette fell out of her mouth. "Is that—"

"Yeah," Brandon answered.

I stood, staring. The sigil was scratched into the chrome plating of the bumper. I didn't need to see the notebook to know it was identical to the ones on the boulders outside the cave and the one on the Mathesons' cabin. Pain pulsed in my chest and I wondered for a moment what a heart attack felt like.

"How the fuck did it get here?" she asked.

I ran a hand through my hair and tried to hide the tremor in my voice. "Are we sure it wasn't there before?"

"It wasn't there before, Nate." Brandon's voice was grim. "You know what it is. It's *His* sign."

I shook my head. "No. We couldn't find the cave. It can't be real. If it was real, we would've found the cave." I was rambling. None of this made sense anymore.

"Did either of you see or hear anything weird last night?" Brandon asked.

Jennifer pulled the pill bottle from her pocket and shook one out into her palm. "I took something to help me sleep. I didn't see or hear anything."

"Nate, you said you had trouble sleeping. Nightmares?"

I swallowed hard. The relief I'd felt when we failed to find the cave started to melt away. My hands shook and my stomach churned. "Yeah, but it was a dream."

"What kind of dream?" Jennifer asked. The tone of her voice frightened me.

"I went to the cave," I began. "Lee followed me. I saw Him—Forest Man. I took His hand, and then the kids... they sang and danced around me. They were all dead."

Her hand flew over her mouth. "You sent Lee."

"I didn't. I woke up in the cabin. None of it was real!"

Tears flowed down her cheeks. "It was like that with me, too. We told you it came to us in our dreams, but you wouldn't listen! You think you know everything, and you didn't believe us, and you wouldn't listen, and now Lee's dead! He's dead like Franklin and Sarah and Marcus, and you did this!" She pounded her fists against my chest. "How dare you sit back and judge us, acting all high and mighty, and then..." she finished with a sob.

I tried to put an arm around her, but she swatted me away.

"Don't you dare fucking touch me!"

"Jennifer, I—"

She didn't wait to hear my excuses. She stormed off towards the cabin, but she didn't go inside. She crossed the side yard to the back of the building.

Brandon and I followed. He hadn't said anything since my revelation of the nightmare, but I could tell something was on his mind by his furrowed brow.

Jennifer traced her fingers across the window frame. It was Sarah's window. She was searching for the mark. When her hand stopped and she collapsed to her knees, I knew she must've found it.

"I did it," she cried. "I fucking murdered my sister. My parents and my therapists... they all tried to tell me I felt guilty and responsible because I loved her, not because it was my fault. They all told me... bullshit." It was the sound of her heart breaking.

"It isn't true, Jennifer. You know it isn't." I leaned beside her, putting a hand on her shoulder.

She slapped my hand away. "You keep saying that, but everything keeps pointing us back to Forest Man." Her eyes were wide, and her head twitched from side to side. I was losing her.

"I'll prove it isn't true."

She sniffled. "How?"

"I'll find Lee, wherever he's hiding." He had to be lurking somewhere nearby. We hadn't found the cave, which meant I hadn't done anything wrong. None of us had. If finding that asshole was what it took to snap Jennifer back to reality, that's what I was going to do. "Brandon will come with me. Why don't you go back into the cabin and rest for a bit?"

She nodded, but continued staring at the sigil carved in the window frame. "Go ahead. I just need a minute."

I turned to Brandon. "I don't suppose you have any actual lockpicks, do you?"

There was no mirth in his smile. "Why are you always asking me that question? It's like you think the Scouts train people for breaking and entering."

"Well, do you?"

"Of course I do."

I set off towards the nearest cabin, the one that had belonged to Lee's family. It seemed his most likely destination. It was the closest, not to mention the one he'd be most familiar with. Hell, for all I knew, he might even still have a key to it.

CHAPTER 29

Brandon stood at the front door, lockpick in hand. The deck around the cabin had fallen into disrepair. Latticework hung in broken sheets, and several handrails were missing. Even so, there were no broken windows or other signs of vandalism. I supposed rumors about the haunted lake were responsible for that.

"Explain something to me," he said.

I smirked. "Me? Explain something to you? That'd be a first, don't you think?"

"Even so."

I could tell by his tone this was going to be a conversation I didn't want to have. Not yet. Not until we found Lee. "Okay, I'll bite. What would you like me to explain?"

He worked his pick into the lock, applying pressure and lifting the pins. "I know you don't want to scare Jennifer. I get it, but you know as well as I do what that sigil on Lee's truck means. You know he's gone."

I shifted uncomfortably.

"There it is." He turned the knob, swinging the door open. "If you dreamed about the cave, and Lee is missing, then it means you left something that belonged to Lee for *Him*."

"It was a dream!"

"What did you leave?"

"God damn it!" I kicked the door frame, sending a jolt of pain through my foot.

"Nate, we can't keep playing this game indefinitely. We're going to run out of places to look, and every time you lead her in the wrong direction, she's going to wander further from your reach."

"It isn't about that," I said, taking a look around the sitting room. There were sheets of plastic covering the furniture. The cabin was frozen in time, waiting for the family to come back and spend the summer.

"I think that's exactly what this is about. You need to tell her. Stop trying to erase it, and deal with it."

Wetness streaked down my cheeks. "She's never going to forgive me for Lee, is she?"

"Hard to say," he answered.

"I left his lighter."

Brandon turned his calm but solemn gaze on me, but I couldn't meet his eyes.

"I found it when we were kids, and I picked it up. Held onto it. So many times over the years I thought about throwing it away, but I couldn't. When I knew we were coming back, I packed it. I don't even know why."

Brandon nodded once. "Let's go back and find her, okay?"

I swallowed the lump in my throat, and wiped my eyes. "Yeah, okay."

CHAPTER 30

Brandon stopped halfway across the yard.

"What?" I asked, halting mid-stride behind him.

He pointed at Lee's truck. "The doors are open."

"And?"

"I closed them after I found his stash."

I stepped towards the truck. "See? He's back! I told you this was ridiculous. Man, you almost had me believing this whole thing, too." I peered inside. The glove box was open, and papers were strewn across the dashboard.

"The drugs are gone," Brandon said.

"Yeah, well, did you doubt he was going to come back for them? I mean, that shit's expensive." I gestured towards the empty box.

"He wouldn't trash his own truck," Brandon said, holding up a wad of papers in his hand.

"Shit."

"Shit indeed," Brandon agreed, and we took off for the cabin at a sprint.

"Jennifer!" I flung the door open and crossed the kitchen in three strides. "Jennifer! Where are you?"

I knocked on her bedroom door. "Jennifer? Are you in there?" I pressed my ear against the door. There was no answer.

Brandon made his way down the hall, stopping to open every door.

The knob to her door wouldn't budge. "Brandon! She's locked in!"

"Fuck!" Brandon looked down at the knob. "We'll kick it in."

I nodded.

"On three."

"One."

"Two."

We kicked and the door gave way, sending shards of broken wood flying. Jennifer was on the bed, her face translucent. I placed my head against her chest.

"Is she breathing?" Brandon asked.

"I can't tell!"

He pushed me aside and placed two fingers on her neck.

I glanced around the room frantically. Orange bottles littered the floor. I picked one up and examined it. Oxy. "Shit. It's empty. How many do you think she took?"

I sat on the edge of the bed and took her hand in mine. Her skin was cold and oddly clammy. Her lips were blue along the edges and a thin layer of drool ran down her cheek onto the pillow beneath her.

"She has a pulse. If you have a cell signal, call an ambulance."

I nodded and lit up my phone. No service. I shook my head at Brandon.

"Pick her up," he ordered, his Eagle Scout instincts taking over. "Put her in the Jeep. Climb in back with her, I'll get us to the ER."

I hugged her frail body to my chest as I carried her out of the cabin. As I stepped over the threshold with her in my arms, I thought how differently this trip had played out in my mind. I'd wanted to give her closure, to help her start over, but I'd only pushed her over the edge.

I climbed into the back seat and cradled her head in my lap, unable to hold back the sobs that wracked my chest.

CHAPTER 31

The scent of disinfectant mingled with something I couldn't place, giving the hospital a distinct smell. A smell I'd always associated with sick people. The stark walls and fluorescent lights made the whole place feel cliché, the way a person imagined a hospital should look.

Brandon entered the room juggling two paper coffee cups and a white bag. "You haven't had a proper meal in at least a day," he said, offering me the bag.

I opened to find an everything bagel with cream cheese. "Thanks, man." I pulled the shrink wrap off and took a bite. I felt guilty, eating while Jennifer lay there, hooked up to all those machines.

"She's going to pull through."

I nodded. "The doctor said after they've finished running tests, they'll probably transfer her to the psych ward. She'll probably be there a few days for observation." I sat the rest of the bagel back down on the bag and took her hand in mine.

It was limp, but some of the color had come back to her skin. She looked sickly, though less like a corpse.

A throat clearing in the doorway made me sit back and pull my hand away. A woman in her late fifties or early sixties stepped into the room. I hadn't seen her in years, but the resemblance was still there. It was Jennifer's mother.

"Mrs. Davis. It's been a long time."

Her attention was drawn to the form that lay on the bed. For a moment, I wasn't sure she'd even heard me speak, but finally she replied. "I remember you, Nathan Holbrook. Jennifer used to talk about you all the time. She was really quite enamored of you when you two were children."

I flushed, but remained silent. I didn't trust myself to answer.

I needn't have worried, because she continued, "She never did get over losing Sarah. She's always blamed herself. She's been through so much." The woman stepped forward and brushed a strand of hair out of Jennifer's face. "You two were with her when this happened." It wasn't a question.

"Yes, Ma'am," Brandon answered anyway.

"Seeing the two of you must have brought back painful memories for her." She settled down into a chair beside the bed.

I suddenly felt like an intruder, both in this room and in her life. I knew virtually nothing about her as an adult, and yet I'd marched in, arrogant and certain I could fix it, fix *her*. I hadn't considered for a moment if she'd even needed fixing.

I grabbed the bagel and my coffee, and stood. "Mrs. Davis, would you mind if I come back to visit?"

She nodded, fluffing the pillow under Jennifer's head. "Anytime. I'm sure she'll appreciate it. After these episodes... well, that's when she needs friends and family the most."

Episodes. My eyes flitted to the scars on her wrists. I wiped away unshed tears and headed out the door with Brandon.

EPILOGUE

"Nate?"

The pounding on my apartment door matched the pounding ache of my head. An empty rum bottle sat on the coffee table in front of me along with a collection of other half-filled bottles of booze. I was wearing yesterday's clothes. The day before that too, possibly. All the days blurred into one long nightmare. I couldn't remember anymore.

"Coming." I pushed myself off the couch and to the door. I hadn't locked it. Anyone could have walked right in. I turned the knob, and Dr. Coleridge stood in the hallway. "Susan. What are you doing here?"

Her glasses rested on her forehead, holding back a wave of gray curls. She wore black slacks with a freshly pressed shirt and smelled vaguely of vanilla and lavender. Her leather briefcase hung at her side.

"I haven't seen you on campus," she said.

"I'm taking a sabbatical," I answered. "Would you like to come in?"

"Yes, please."

I grimaced and held the door open wider. I had hoped she'd say no.

Her eyes wandered from surface to surface. I could feel the weight of her thoughts as she put together the puzzle in her mind. Her eyes stopped on the row of bottles on the table. "I was concerned about you, Nate. Is everything okay?"

"You wouldn't believe me if I told you," I muttered.

"What's that?" she asked.

"A friend of mine..." I started, then choked on something from deep-down. "Jennifer. You met her at your office. She's in the hospital. She tried to commit..."

I couldn't say it. Just like with Forest Man, I was too much of a coward to say the words, but Susan understood the weight of my silence.

"I'm sorry to hear that."

From the tone of her voice and the way her eyes searched the shadows, it was apparent that she had learned something.

"Nate, I'm actually here because of what you brought me. I've done a lot of digging since you and your friends came to my office. I think I know what that symbol is, and how it connects to your stump man."

"Forest Man." I reached for one of the bottles and filled a dirty glass with amber liquid.

"Pardon?"

I emptied the glass in one gulp. "Its name is Forest Man. It takes people. Children mostly, but sometimes grownups, too."

I ushered her in, then shut the door against the night.

"Sit down, Susan, I have a story to tell you."

ACKNOWLEDGMENTS

I owe many people a debt of gratitude in the making and writing of this book. I would not have had the courage to start writing, or to do much else with my life, without the influence of my husband, Chris. I would not be a writer if it weren't for his patience and encouragement, and our weekly trips to coffee shops for "writing dates."

For reading through multiple drafts and always providing comments and suggestions with kindness and wisdom, I'd like to thank Austin Shirley and Kali White VanBaale. This book was shaped by their input and suggestions. Characters grew and changed through their influence, and the result is a much better story. Kali served as the advisor for my master's thesis, during which time I took a short story called "Forest Man," and turned it into the novella you now hold in your hand. Kali's guidance throughout the process made me feel confident in my ability to work in this longer form, something I'd never done before.

Thanks also to Michelle River for believing in me and taking a chance on me when I was new to writing and needed it the most. You were my first publisher, but now I'm proud to also call you my friend.

A special thank you, and my unending gratitude to D. Alexander Ward and the folks over at *Bleeding Edge Books* for not only believing in this little book, but also working through edits, arranging cover art, and always being on top of everything throughout the process. It's scary to be a new author, but *Bleeding Edge Books* made the process easy, and renewed my excitement and enthusiasm for the story.

ABOUT THE AUTHOR

HOLLEY CORNETTO is a writer, librarian, professor, book reviewer, and transplanted southerner who now calls New Jersey home. Her short fiction has appeared in magazines such as Daily Science Fiction, Flame Tree Press Newsletter, Dark Recesses Press, and anthologies from Cemetery Gates Media, Eerie River Publishing, and Dark Ink Press. In 2020, she was awarded a grant from the Ladies of Horror Fiction. In addition to writing *The Horror Tree*'s weekly newsletter, she regularly reviews for *Booklist, Ginger Nuts of Horror, and Dark Recesses Press*. She teaches creative writing in the online MFA program at Southern New Hampshire University, as well as composition at County College of Morris. Find her on Twitter @HLCornetto.